COMPLICATED SHADOWS

BOOKS BY JAMES D.F. HANNAH

The Henry Malone novels
Midnight Lullaby
Complicated Shadows
She Talks To Angels
Friend of the Devil
Behind the Wall of Sleep

The Parker County novels
The Righteous Path

JAMES D.F. HANNAH

COMPLICATED SHADOWS

A Henry Malone Novel

First Down & Out Books Edition March 2021

Down & Out Books
3959 Van Dyke Road, Suite 265
Lutz, FL 33558
DownAndOutBooks.com

Cover design by Eric Beetner

ISBN: 1-64396-172-1
ISBN-13: 978-1-64396-172-9

To my grandfather, John B.

CHAPTER 1

Billy helped get me the job, a fact I wasn't ready to forgive him for.

See, after things had settled following everything with the National Brotherhood, what with this band of white supremacists falling apart, some folks getting arrested, other folks getting killed, and the Feds bulldozing the compound into a blank space in the middle of nowhere, I found myself with too much time on my hands.

Beforehand, I'd have been okay with it, since I had a disability retirement from the state police thanks to the shotgun blast that had left me with a gimpy knee. The thing was, I'd rediscovered the joy of getting off of my ass and doing things again, even if some of those things had almost gotten me killed. Still, the whole clusterfuck had opened up a desire to be a productive member of society again. I gave it a little while to see if any of it passed, like a cold or a case of the shits. When it didn't, I decided I'd better find a job.

Billy Malone—who's had the misfortune of being my father for 42 years—had retired from the coal mines years ago, but he still knew people, and among those people was a guy who needed someone to work security at a strip mine. It might have sounded fun, but it shouldn't have, because it wasn't.

The job put me at the front gate of Witcher Shoals Mine #4, where my main priority was to make sure the gate rose and dropped when folks swiped their electronic pass across the scanner, and to shoo away protesters if they violated the hundred-yard limit. There'd been folks with their panties in a bunch over strip mining operations, based on the idea they didn't think blowing up the tops of mountains and turning it into flat land was a good thing.

I should have an opinion on the whole thing; I had watched my coffee cup dance across the tabletop following some earth-shattering kabooms—explosions that sheared more rock from a mountaintop in the search for coal. Sometimes an explosion let loose a chunk of mountain that took out a house or some cars. No one had been hurt yet, but you had to wonder how long luck like that could last.

I can't say I was a big fan of the landscape left behind. All of this work knocked the mountains into barren nubs, shorn of century-old growth, empty for years until reclamation work came around and rolled out grass deer ate within weeks, and planted trees that would take decades to grow.

Losing the mountains also gave way to views of the horizon none of us knew what to do with. We'd grown up with mountains surrounding us, enclosing and encasing us, keeping us safe from the outside world and the 21st century. Before you knew it, we'd have a clear view of Ohio, and no one wanted that shit.

But I wasn't smart enough to figure out a better option, either. The world wanted coal—if less of it than in years prior—and the universe had seen fit to shove it into seams not easily reached through conventional means. Plus, Parker County needed the jobs; nobody else was asking us to dance, and you couldn't expect anyone to keep their family fed wearing a blue vest and stocking shelves.

Long story short, I suppose, was I had a job. It was early May, but the weather was already hot as the crotch of flannel boxers at the equator, and the little box they put me in didn't have air conditioning. I did have a fan which pushed warm, thick air around, and the ultimate effect was like getting smacked in the face with a wet towel.

The company gave me a pale blue polo shirt with a badge stitched on where a pocket should have been, a nightstick, and a can of pepper spray. I spent the days sitting in the little box, waving through miners who drove in and out for their shifts, and reading. Woody, my AA sponsor, had given me a copy of *The Big Sleep*, by Raymond Chandler. I'd heard of the movie, had never seen it, and didn't realize there was a book. Woody said I should read up on the basics and aim to become a shamus. I'd laughed, then went home and Googled what "shamus" meant.

The sun was up, and the early morning rays beat down on us like we owed them money. Mist hung from what remained of the mountaintops, clinging to the trees like cobwebs. You learned to dread humidity like that. It was a sign that the day would get oppressive. I hoped the air conditioner in my shit-hole trailer kept working.

The plan was to go home and try to sleep, most likely with Izzy next to me. Izzy was the Shetland pony-sized bullmastiff who kept reign over my house. I'd had her since coming back to Parker County, when Woody told me I needed something to care about besides myself. She kept me decent company if you counted snoring as company.

I worked the job with another guard, and his job was to periodically patrol the grounds on a four-wheeler. Mitchell was an older guy, built like the Southern sheriff from every movie made in the 1970s, all chest and torso and attitude, with gray-white hair growing out in tufts aimed in every direction. He had more gut than shirt, and the bottom of the shirt was always coming out from the waist of his polyester slacks, and he forever had his hand down the front of his pants, tucking the shirt back in. At least, that's all I thought he was doing. He had his hand down there often enough, he could be checking for lumps. He was in the midst of doing just that when he walked up to the box as our shifts were about to end.

Mitchell finished ball-checking like he was Michael Jordan

and whipped his cell phone from his back pocket.

"You see those naked pictures of the chick from that movie?" he said. He smiled and licked his lips, and I felt a bubble of bile reach up through my throat.

"You're gonna have to narrow it down," I said. "I'm trying to think of actresses who haven't had photos of everything they've got show up."

He danced his thumb across the screen. "This young one, she's gotta be about my daughter's age. Real hot piece of ass."

The bile threatened to charge further, and I worked to keep it at bay. "Mitchell, that statement's fucked up for so many reasons, I'd have to diagram the ways it's wrong," I said. "Thanks for the generous offer, but no, I don't want to see them."

He furrowed his eyebrows together. They were hairy little fuckers, and knitted together they made him look like a missing evolutionary step.

"You a fag or something?" he said.

"No, I'm not, and it'd be none of your goddamn business if I was, anyway," I said. "But I don't get off on pictures of a naked chick when I'm not the one she's taking a picture for. I would prefer to see a real woman who wants me to see her naked."

Mitchell laughed. "Goddamn, you are a fag. She's some Hollywood slut, that's all. They put their shit up there on the screen all the time."

Coming up from the distance, I saw my shift replacement walking toward the guard station. I checked my watch. Three minutes 'til seven.

Goddamn close enough for me.

I said, "I'm out of here. But I hope you enjoy staring at daughter-aged starlet ass."

I got out of the box and said "hey" to my replacement. He was a young guy named Plants, and our only interaction was uttering that "hey" to one another every morning when he took over the next shift. He nodded in my direction, and we moved on through our lives. It was a beneficial arrangement that worked for us.

I headed to the main office to clock out and glanced back. Mitchell leaned through the box window, showing Plants his phone, and laughing.

CHAPTER 2

It was Tuesday, which was my de facto Friday. Even though my job involved doing equal amounts of jack and shit, I needed the next two days off. I didn't feel the greatest, and if I didn't know better, I'd have thought I was coming down with something, but this was one of those rare moments where I knew better.

Part of the problem was I was still married, at least in the legal sense. Maggie had left Morgantown and taken a job with a newspaper in Philadelphia. It was getting harder to not sign the divorce papers. We hadn't seen one another in more than a year, when I'd gone up to Morgantown one weekend, and she'd made it clear she wasn't interested in trying. We still talked, sometimes not even about divorce, but if you had to narrow down most of our conversations, that would have been the most frequent topic.

I'd made a go at dating. Her name was Doria, and things didn't work out well after white supremacists kidnapped her and she got shot in the leg and decided I wasn't worth the effort. I couldn't say I blamed her, but in my defense, I wasn't the one who had shot her, and her getting shot had probably saved her life. There's just no talking to some people, I suppose.

I sat in my car, tapping my fingers across the steering wheel. It was five after seven.

I could hear Woody's voice in the back of my head, telling me I should go to a meeting. I'm not sure why I'd want to listen to him, though; he'd been the one who shot Doria. I could have argued he was part of the problem.

There was the eight o'clock meeting at St. Anthony's. *Why not?* I thought. I could always use the coffee.

Folks hung outside the church entrance, smoking and bullshitting, both vital to AA meetings. I pulled my car between faded yellow lines as my cell phone rang. I didn't recognize the number and let it go to voicemail. Odds were it was a bill collector, and I didn't feel like lying to anyone that early in the day.

Woody saw me as I walked toward the entrance. He was one of those lean, lanky guys who'd looked 50 since he was 20, but hadn't aged since. He kept his black hair pulled back in a ponytail, and he dressed in black T-shirts and blue jeans, and he looked like he should have been on the poster for the movie *Tombstone*. He'd been my sponsor since I'd moved home. I didn't know much about him, such as why he kept canister grenades in his truck box. Maybe I didn't need to know anything. Maybe I only needed someone to help keep me sober and alive, and his past didn't matter. That he was a general-issue badass and sniper-grade shot didn't hurt, though, and those seemed as good of reasons as any to keep him around.

He handed me a pack of cigarettes and a lighter. I shook seven minutes of my life free, lit it, and took in a lung-deep drag of carcinogens.

"You just off work?" Woody said.

I nodded. "The uniform was a tip off, wasn't it?"

"Thought maybe you just wore it on account it gave you a sense of power of authority."

"Men tremble at the sight of me, and women crumble to my feet. Truth told, I didn't feel like going home and staring at the TV or the dog."

"The dog might miss you."

"The dog is the one creature on this planet who I guarantee misses me."

"Yet here you are, amid the bungled and the botched."

"Like you always tell me: a dollar here buys you all the coffee and human misery a man could ever want."

"Where else you gonna get that value for your money?" He took a last pull of his cigarette and crushed it underneath the scuffed toe of his Doc Martens. "Come on and let's listen to everyone bitch."

Morning meetings run on the small side, because people have jobs and lives, and they don't want to be up that early if they don't need to be. This meeting had a dozen or so in it, and they were long-timers. You got a lot of shift workers in morning meetings, and I recognized a guy from the mines across the table from me. We gathered in one of the Sunday school rooms. I poured myself a cup of coffee, dumped sugar and powdered creamer in there, and hoped for the best.

We went around the room, one by one, talking about what we had going on in our lives and what we were doing to not be drinking. When it got to me, I said, "Hi, my name's Henry, and I'm an alcoholic. Today, I'm happy to not be drinking, because it doesn't get me anywhere. It's not solving my problems. It's not fixing anything with me that's broken. I miss it, and I hate people who can do it without their lives turning into disasters, but I can't, so I'm content to be here, to be sober, and taking it a day at a time." I let it move on to the person next to me.

After the meeting, once we all got started smoking again, and Woody said, "Talk to Maggie?"

"No."

"How long you plan on dodging the inevitable?".

"I figure I might have another 30, 35 years ahead of me. I think I can pull off at least another 10 before she gets too upset."

Woody inhaled off of his cigarette. He held it between his forefinger and thumb as he drew the smoke in and let it out.

"You are a fucking asshole," he said.

"Seems to be the consensus."

Woody finished his cigarette. "I'm headed over to the Riverside to get breakfast. Want to join?"

I shook my head. "I've got to let Izzy out. I'd wager she's bouncing around the inside of the house with her legs crossed, and she's got bladder enough, if she lets loose, it'll flood the place."

"Call me later, then. Come by and we'll shoot things."

Woody had built his own range behind his house, and put in regular efforts to make me a better shot. Things were improving, but there'd be seismic shifts and political revolutions happening quicker than me hitting a bull's-eye anytime soon.

Back in my car, I checked my phone. Whoever had called before the meeting had left a message.

"Henry, it's Pete Calhoun. I'm in Parker County for a few days and wanted to see if you wanted to grab a bite to eat, have a beer. I'm staying at the Days Inn near the One Stop. Gimme a call. It's been a month of Tuesday since I seen ya, since...well, since what shit happened. I'll even buy the first round. Later, tater."

There's nothing like a voice from the past to make life drop on you like test results from the doctor.

CHAPTER 3

Pete Calhoun and I had been stationed at the same state police detachment when we were troopers. He was a bear in people's clothes, a giant, lumbering dude who looked like the friendliest guy you'd never want to fight with. He worked a desk most of that time, with him pushing paperwork and making duty rosters and other general issue office bullshit. You were almost court-mandated to like Pete: he knew the dirtiest jokes, gave everyone a decent amount of hell but treated them fair, and he took the job seriously, but he never let it drag him down the way some of us did.

I heard from Pete after I got shot and left the force. The calls and emails dwindled off, though, because we were guys, and "out of sight, out of mind" is one of our primary settings, and I had turned into a reminder people didn't want to hear, a warning they didn't want to have to heed.

I got home and let Izzy out and watched her squat in about a hundred different locations, squeezing out droplets of moisture to make sure every inch of the grass was marked. We went back inside and turned on the AC. It was a wall unit I'd shoved into a bedroom window. It sputtered and coughed and the motor whined like a four-year-old who wasn't getting candy at the store. I pounded at the top of the unit up and it made one last protest before stirring to life and pushing out cold air.

I stripped down to my boxers and climbed into bed. I laid

there for a while, throwing myself around the mattress, trying to sleep and failing. Izzy stretched out on top of the covers beside me, because letting her underneath would have been weird, right? She snored, her fat lips flapping and showing off teeth the size of drywall screws. I wondered if I should have the goddamn beast checked for sleep apnea.

My work uniform rested in a pile in a corner. I stared in its direction and tried to will it to burst into flames. It didn't happen. Pyrokinesis wasn't in the cards for me.

I hated that uniform. I hated the sewn-on badge, like it made you look official, instead of being a douche with a fabric shield on your chest. I hated how the polyester slacks pulled at my crotch, shifting my junk around and making my balls ache. But more than anything, I hated how it reminded me I wasn't a cop anymore, and now I didn't have a clue who the fuck I was supposed to be, or what the fuck to do with myself anymore.

I'd worked myself into a fine lather of self-loathing by the time my cell phone rang. It was Pete. I laid there staring at the ceiling as I answered.

"Hey, boss," I said.

"Morning there, man. You could return a man's calls, he bothers to look your sorry ass up."

"Busy social calendar, Pete. So many people, so little time." I sat up in bed. Izzy opened one eye, made sure I wasn't going anywhere, and rolled over on her back. "What the hell are you doing in Serenity? There's no good reason to be here unless you're trapped here like the rest of us."

"Way to sell the town, Malone. You working for the tourism board now? Maybe the chamber of commerce?"

"No one comes to Parker County without a motive, Pete."

"True enough. You feel like breakfast, maybe an early lunch, and we can catch up?"

My alarm clock read six minutes after 10. I'd been awake since noon the day before. My body ached for sleep, but my brain was too restless to relax, which was funny since no one had ever accused me of thinking too much.

"Wanna say 11?" I said. "There's a place, O'Dell's, in downtown, or whatever constitutes downtown for Serenity. It's easy to find."

"Awesome, possum. See you then."

I hung up the phone and planted my feet on the floor and headed for the bathroom to shower.

O'Dell's is a sports bar close to the Parker County courthouse. You run across a lot of attorneys and judges and courthouse workers there, especially after work hours, when they throw back a few and find new lies to tell. It gets obnoxious then, with egos knocking against one another, and toxic levels of bullshit spewed. But the cheeseburgers are good, and the waffle fries have bay seasoning on them, so you took the good with the bad.

I could have met Pete at the Riverside, but Woody would still have an AA crew there, doing one of his epic coffee klatches, and I wasn't in a mood where I wanted my worlds to mix—the cop life I'd had before, and the sober-yet-grumpy-retirement life I had now. A therapist would have said I was compartmentalizing; the therapist would have been correct.

Pete was sipping a Michelob Ultra when I got there. He got up and gave me a hug so manly it made Chuck Norris look like a crossdresser.

"Goddamn but you've gotten fatter and uglier since I saw you," he said as he nearly cracked my ribs.

Pete had bulked up himself, and had gone gray in the process, his bristly crew cut the color of gunmetal. There was a thick wedge of hair shoved beneath a wide, flat nose, and it compounded with the girth to make him look like a friendly walrus.

Once he let me go, I subtly made sure nothing was broken, and we sat down. The waitress came over and handed me a menu. I ordered a Coke, and she left.

Pete said, "A Coke? I remember days of you doing Jaeger

bombs for breakfast. You getting your pussy waxed later, too?"

I took a deep breath and said, "I quit drinking."

Pete gave a nod and sipped his beer. "I got ya. I don't drink anymore. Course, I don't drink any less either." He busted out into a huge laugh, since it had to be the first time I'd heard the joke. Then he turned serious. "You serious? You quit drinking?"

"Serious as a heart attack. I got sober and got into AA."

His expression said he had nothing to do with this information, so he took another drink of his beer. "Good for you, then. Some friends of mine, they've done AA, and it's good for them. You mind me drinking?"

"Have at it. I just won't be having any."

Pete finished the beer and, when the waitress brought me my Coke, he asked for another. He ordered chicken strips, and I got a cheeseburger with jalapeños and fries.

I drank some Coke. "Life looks like it's treating you well," I said.

"Can't complain. I retired about a year back. I'd done my time, and I could get out with a full pension. I was tired of sitting at a desk all day anyway, figured I'd find something else to get into."

There was a wedding ring on his left hand. Pete's hands were huge, rough, and dark from time in the sun. The ring was simple, a gold band bought when he'd been a few pounds lighter, and now it was tight around the digit, and not going to go anywhere.

"You get married?" I said. "I'd figured you for the lifelong bachelor."

He gave the ring a twist and moved his face around into a lopsided smile. "Yeah, I took the plunge. It's good, but we hit a rough patch. I'm not sure what will happen." There was a strain in his voice, an effort to shift conversational gears. "What about you and Maggie? You kids got any little ones yet?"

"I guess this is where it's my turn to let things get awkward," I said. "Maggie and I aren't together anymore. She stayed in Morgantown, and she's in Philadelphia now. She's the web editor for a newspaper there."

Things got quiet, as things do when we discuss our failures. I ran my finger across the rim of my glass.

"So how you killing those long hours spent not busting humps? Sit at home, watch the Game Show Network? Go fishing? Got yourself a garden? Because I don't see you out there hauling dirt around, fussing over flowers."

"I did the fishing thing, until I couldn't stand sitting on my ass all day waiting for something to happen. Hell, 30 years with the state police was enough of that shit. No, I went and got myself a private investigator's license."

"You get a trench coat and fedora with that?"

Pete laughed. "I'll tell you what; it's not a bad way to kill time you got that refuses to die."

"What kind of shit you doing?"

"A little of this, a little of that. I do contract work for an agency, most of it your basic stuff, like working insurance cases, running security for events. What you up to?"

"Security for a coal company now."

The waitress brought us our food. Pete flipped open the lid on the ketchup bottle and squeezed until his French fries had vanished underneath an ocean of red. "You working out of the box at the entrance?"

"Generally. My knee doesn't give me much allowance for running around."

"I could see where that would be a problem." Pete took a bite of chicken strip. "You like it?"

"No. It sucks sweaty ball sack, actually, but it's what's there for the time being."

"After all the shit with the white supremacists, I thought you'd get famous there for a hot minute. No book deals, maybe a TV movie?"

"Not the kind of famous I want to be."

"Famous is famous, isn't it? What other kinds of famous are there?"

I bit into my burger. The jalapeños were fresh, and I felt a good burn as I chewed. I sipped my Coke. "There's famous for helping bust up a white supremacist organization, and there's famous for dragging a massive dick around on a roller skate. I'd prefer the 'massive dick' kind of famous."

Pete motioned to the waitress, and she brought him over a fresh beer. He drank some.

"Most of what I end up doing is divorce work, or background checks, the crap big firms don't wanna deal with, or it's too little for them to hassle," he said. "I make fifty an hour doing shit anyone with Google can do."

He stood up enough to reach into his front jeans pocket and bring out a small case, flipped it open and handed me a business card. It looked professional, glossy with raised letters.

"'Peter Calhoun, Security and Investigations,'" I said. "Check you out."

"Don't let it get your dick too hard. Those are ten bucks for a shit-ton of them from a place online. It's not like the old days with Jim Rockford, he had the little printing press set up in his car, making 'em up as he went."

I set the card on the table. "Still don't explain what you're doing in Parker County. It's not like you came for the view, or for the scintillating nightlife."

He picked up a chicken strip, looked at it, set it back down. "I'm looking for a guy named Isaac Martin. He's from around here, and I thought you might help."

"In spite of what you might have heard, we're not all related around here."

Pete took a drink of his beer. "I saw a T-shirt a couple of years ago that said 'It's All Relative in West Virginia.'"

"Yeah, it's like the one for Kentucky: 'Three Million People, 15 Last Names,'" I said. "Because if you can't laugh at incest, what can you laugh at?"

CHAPTER 4

Isaac Martin was a programmer for a tech startup in Morgantown. Red Salt LLC was three friends from West Virginia University who had gotten together and developed a digital currency similar to Bitcoin. What I understood about Bitcoin was no one understood the shit, but the news channels liked to talk about it. What I got was that it some monetary system where you purchased the currency to use in online transactions.

"Red Salt developed Cashbyte," Pete said. "Everything so far is just the 'hype' stage, where people talk, but the infrastructure isn't secure yet. But they're getting big about it. The hype's enough where you have countries in Central and South America talking about switching to Cashbyte as a national currency because they can't manage their own."

"I'd like to apologize now for only understanding about a third of what you're talking about," I said. "I'll nod a lot, if that's okay."

"I can't make much sense of it, either. You've got to be a combination of financial expert and computer nerd to follow it all."

"How rich is any of this making Martin?"

"So far, it's not. But it almost doesn't matter because they've got people lining up to throw money behind the damn thing. The company's building name recognition, and people say it's more stable than Bitcoin, which is a big selling point. The thing with Bitcoin is you can buy it and the value fluctuates for no reason; it's like putting a fifty in your wallet before you go to bed at night and waking up the next day and you've got yourself either a hundred or a twenty. Cashbyte holds its value, which makes it less of a financial gamble."

My head ached as I tried to think about it. I drank more of my Coke.

"When did Martin disappear?" I said.

"A week ago. Red Salt was scheduled to meet with a group of backers—Japanese businessmen who wanted to invest—and Martin never showed up for the meeting."

"And no clue where he went?"

"He wouldn't be 'missing' if someone knew where he was, would he?"

Pete reached into a briefcase next to his chair and brought out an iPad. He flicked at the screen and pulled up a photo of Martin.

Isaac Martin was so boyish-looking, he'd get carded until his 40s. He was thin and tan and spent time in a gym. His blonde hair was stylish, cut short on the sides and back and longer on top, and his teeth couldn't have been whiter if he brushed with Clorox. The photo was from a beach vacation, where Martin wore a Hawaiian shirt, standing in one of those restaurants where life is a constant luau. Someone's arm was around his shoulder, but the picture was cropped to show only Martin.

"He doesn't look like a guy who spends his life in front of a computer," I said.

Pete glanced at the iPad. "No, I don't suppose he does."

"And what makes you think he came back to Parker County?"

"Nothing except I've got nothing else to go on. His parents are dead, and there's no other family. He hasn't touched his bank accounts and credit cards since he vanished."

"Any chance he's been moving his own money into Cashbyte or some other one of the electronic currency things?"

Pete shook his head. "Nothing from his financials for the

past year shows anything like that."

"What about friends? He got a wife or a girlfriend?"

"Neither," Pete slipped the iPad back inside his briefcase. He hadn't finished his food, but he still pushed away the half-full plate. "I need help here. You're a familiar face in these parts, so they may be more open with you than with me." Pete tapped his thumb on the tabletop. "I'll throw part of my fee towards you, obviously. I need to find the guy."

I scribbled my email address on the back of the business card he'd given me and handed it to him. "Email me what you have and let me see what I can find out. Give me a day."

"I can ask for little else."

"Good, because since you're on an expense account, you're buying lunch."

CHAPTER 5

Pete didn't have much on Martin. Only that Martin graduated from Parker County High School a decade prior, ran off to WVU, scored himself a degree in computer programming, and started up Red Salt with some classmates.

I found articles about Cashbyte that touted it as "the next 'currency of the future'" and Red Salt as the "company that would save crypto-currency." You live long enough, you lose count of the things that are "the whatever of the future.'" I still wanted those flying cars and off-world colonies *Blade Runner* promised.

The articles talked about how three programmers from West Virginia had written code which offered not only more security and anonymity than Bitcoin but also simplified the "mining" process, which was the method of how Cashbyte was distributed. It required less computing power and made it more open to more people with fewer resources.

All of this might as well have been in a foreign language; my knowledge of high finance ended with me tossing spare change into a coffee can in the kitchen at night.

Martin's partners in the venture were Patrick Price and Vikram Kaur. In the pictures, Martin looked ill at ease, as though the attention made him nauseous, or nervous.

Price looked less like what I expected a computer programmer to look like, and more like someone who helped blondes do keg stands. He was built like a gym rat, with a neck as thick as a fireplace log, holding up a head like an inverted teardrop. He cropped his hair close to mask a receding hairline and overcompensated with a thick beard and biceps ready to pop the seams of his shirt, compressed into an undersized frame that meant he needed help to reach shit on a tall shelf.

Kaur possessed a casual smile and a lack of guile the other two lacked. He wore glasses with chunky black frames and different T-shirts with smart-assed sayings. In one photo, there was a laser pistol and the words “Han Shot First”; in another, there was a jumbled Rubik’s Cube and “If You’ve Got a Problem, Yo, I’ll Solve It.” He’d wear on a human’s nerves in 30 seconds flat.

Once upon a time, I might have opened the phone book and called up anyone with the name Martin until I tracked down one of his relatives, who I would hope would point me somewhere in his direction. But the problem was we now existed in the 21st century, and even in somewhere as rural as Parker County, no one used phone books anymore, and damn few folks had landlines that would be in the phone book, anyway.

I wish I could say I figured this out early, but I’d be lying if I did. No, instead, I walked to the library, down the street from the courthouse, and found the most recent Parker County phone directory and two pages of listings for the last name “Martin.” On a whim, I looked for my name and saw I wasn’t in there, which made sense since I only had a cell phone. From there I put two and two together, because I’m a goddamn trained investigator.

If Martin was only 10 years out of the local school system, there might be a teacher from Parker County High who remembered him. If they did, they may steer me to family faster than the phone calls.

The Parker County High yearbook for the year Martin graduated—Go, Bucs!—was smaller yet slicker than from my high school days, and looked more designed and less tossed together. I flipped through the senior portraits, looking at kids in their dresses and rented tuxes, and thought how unprepared they were for the world awaiting them, with their wispy and ill-advised facial hair, choppy bangs, and eyes that said they knew everything but didn't understand a fucking thing.

I went back into the annuals, checking the two previous years, and then the two years succeeding years, and I still didn't anyone listed as Isaac Martin. I stepped outside and called Pete.

"How positive are you he graduated from Parker County?" I said.

"What I know says he attended Parker County High. Hell, he was an honors student."

"No chance he got home-schooled, or maybe one of those private Christian schools where they tell you the earth is flat and six thousand years old?"

"What are you getting at, Henry?"

"That Isaac Martin wasn't who he said he was."

Pete got quiet. The silence felt heavy and awkward, and I said I'd call him back.

I double-checked the annual from 10 years ago and looked at the senior pictures one by one until I found him. It seemed his photo had been mislabeled. There could have been a typo at the printer's. Perhaps gremlins had switched photos. Who knew?

Isaac Martin was the valedictorian of that graduating class of Parker County High School, except the name underneath his photo was "Isaac McCoy." He had a litany of honors under his name to have shamed a presidential candidate. Debate team. Chess club. Chemistry club. All-county band. Honor societies with Latin names I couldn't decode with the ring from "Little Orphan Annie" and three good hints. Newspaper editor. Oh, and yearbook editor.

That cut down the chances of a typographical error. Which likely meant Isaac McCoy had opted to become Isaac Martin.

Flipping through the yearbook, Martin was everywhere. There was a game of "Where's Isaac?" on every page. He was in nearly every photo for every group the school offered, and always with this massive smile on his face. He seemed to have legitimately enjoyed the high school experience.

I kind of hated him already.

CHAPTER 6

School consolidations had rolled around to Parker County several years back, the product of a declining student enrollment combined with buildings dating back to the New Deal. My old high school ended up converted into school board offices and training facilities while they built a new high school a few miles up the road. The new building was shaped like a tweaked-out amoeba, with the sense the architect wanted something that seemed "modern" and "art déco" but instead looked like from a 1930s Commander Cody movie serial, constructing the concept of the future on a budget.

Nothing makes you consider your years faster than walking into a high school in your 40s. All around you is nothing but the rushed footsteps of youth and the impatient heartbeat of un-promised tomorrows. You're invisible to these kids, because when they look at you, they have to confront the idea their futures won't be gleaming and shiny, and they may have to settle for less than the perfect dreams they've set for themselves. The curse of youth is you can only imagine a perfect future, so you opt to ignore adults who wear failure in pained strides and second-hand clothing and lined faces and prematurely graying hair, and you tell yourself you'll be different, you'll be better than them.

Fuck them, I thought, as I headed into the front office.

The office felt like the return area at a department store, with chairs against the wall, a long counter on the far end, and several women busy on telephones and computers. A skinny kid sat in a chair with his head between knobby knees. He lifted his head up and stared at me. He looked as though he wanted to vomit. I tried to not take it personally.

The door flew open behind me as I walked toward the counter, and an unstable set of molecules bonded together to resemble a 17-year-old girl burst into the room, blew past me like a tornado aimed at a trailer park, and leaned herself against the counter until most of her torso crossed the countertop. She wasn't much more than a pile of blonde hair and too-tan skin, dressed in denim shorts long enough to make her street legal.

A woman behind the counter was on the telephone, saw the girl and smiled something that hinted at familiarity and dread, and held up a finger toward her. The girl sighed and spun around and rolled her eyes. She looked at me, gave me an appraising once-over, and decided I hadn't been worth the effort. She reached into her back pocket and texted on a smartphone larger than my first television.

The woman hung up the telephone and approached the desk. She was pear-shaped, with white-blonde hair sprayed into a shape high enough to put ceiling fans at risk. She wore drugstore reading glasses pushed above the end of her nose and plum-colored lipstick that matched her nails.

"What is it today, Gloria?" the woman said.

The teen-aged girl finished her text, slipped the phone into her front pocket, and smiled. The blonde woman folded her arms across her ample chest and settled into an expression that said this wasn't her first rodeo.

The girl said, "I need to talk to Dr. Wilder."

"Dr. Wilder is in a meeting right now. Can you tell me what this is about?"

"I need to inform her I graduate next year, and my fascist guidance counselor won't let me sign up for Advanced Placement Physics, and if I don't take this class, I'll never get into an Ivy

League school, and I'll end up at WVU and my life will be nothing but a shattering list of disappointments from then on." She said it all in a way that implied the entire world had gone mad, and she needed someone to set everything right.

The woman went to a computer, tapped on the keyboard, and said, "Your records show you got a C-minus in the standard Physics course." She arched her eyebrows. "That doesn't indicate a grasp of the subject matter needed for AP Physics."

Gloria huffed a breath. "That class was lame. Mrs. Galloway drinks, and she wasn't ever going to give me a good grade, anyway."

"And what makes you think you will do better in AP Physics?"

Gloria cranked her head around at an angle human bones shouldn't allow and cast her eyes toward the heavens. A smile slipped across her face. "Mr. Garson and I, we get along so much better. He's...he's a better instructor, and I'm positive I can bring myself up to the level needed for the class. He...understands me."

The woman fit her lips together into a line so thin and tight, air couldn't have passed through them. "Uh huh. Well, let me tell you what I can do. I will tell Dr. Wilder you came by, and I'll pass this onto her, and she'll decide the best course of action."

Gloria sighed again. She sighed so much, she had to be getting light-headed. "Fine," she said, turning the word into a half-dozen syllables before turning and walking out.

The woman shook her head and said to me, "May I help you?"

"More so than you could her," I said. I identified myself and told her I was an investigator working with a firm out of the Pittsburgh area. It wasn't the most egregious lie I'd tell all day. "I'm looking into a student who attended the high school about 10 years ago, the name of Isaac McCoy."

The woman smiled, an expression more genuine than what Gloria got. "Such a wonderful young man. So smart, so much promise. Has something happened to him?"

"He's missing, and Dr. Wilder might be able to help."

She lifted a partition in the counter and motioned me through. “If you’ll follow me. Dr. Wilder’s office is this way.”

“You told Little Gloria back there Dr. Wilder was in a meeting.”

Her smile turned sharper, and her eyes took on a vague gleam of joyful malevolence. In a tone, and at a volume, intended only for me, she said, “Little Gloria also assumes she can blowjob her way through life, and she will find out when she can’t, that will be the beginning of her shattering list of disappointments.” She returned to her benign expression of feigned pleasantness. “I’ll take you on back to Dr. Wilder.”

CHAPTER 7

Dr. Lillian Wilder was what Woody told me later would be considered "zaftig." I looked the word up and when I realized it essentially meant "curvy," I asked Woody why not say "curvy."

"Because roads are 'curvy,' and no woman wants compared to a road system," he said. "Whereas 'zaftig' sounds exotic, and what woman doesn't want made to feel exotic?"

"That seems complicated as fuck."

"Which is why you're getting divorced, Henry."

Whatever Lillian Wilder was, she looked good. Her dark hair was shoulder-length, and she wore wire-framed glasses. She dressed in a well-tailored turquoise suit with a skirt that exposed enough firm, tanned leg to keep things interesting. I guessed her to be about my age. I could imagine fantasies involving her and being kept after school. I mean, if you're into that kind of thing. Which I am, I suppose.

She came around the desk to meet me and motioned me toward a visitor's chair as she sat back down. I won't act like I didn't watch her walk; it was the best part of my day so far.

She said, "Isaac was one of those students difficult to forget. You know those people who command the room when they enter it, but they never overpower? That was Isaac."

"You couldn't miss him in the yearbook."

"He worked to have a part of everything. In my 20 years in public education, I've found most students try to push through the system and get out into what they tell themselves is the real world, and there's no convincing them how overrated the real world is. Isaac seemed to understand we're only existing moment to moment, and to go with those moments."

"Did you have him in class?"

"I did. I taught English right out of college, and I advised the yearbook staff when they couldn't con anyone else into doing the job. Isaac's graduating class was my last year as adviser, before I finished my doctorate and move into administration."

"Have you ever spoken to Isaac since he graduated?"

"I've had no reason to. I'm not sure what his high school life can tell you."

"Anything would be more than the nothing I'm working with. I guess I'm grasping at straws."

Wilder tented her fingers together and leaned forward, propping her elbows on her desk. "The best way to put this, Mr. Malone, is, yes, Isaac was popular, but Isaac wasn't what you'd term 'well-liked.' Those two terms aren't exclusive to one another when dealing with teenagers."

"I remember high school well enough to understand the process is a shark tank and everyone has a bleeding wound."

"Let me assure you that in the age of social media, everything has gotten worse. But 10 years ago, it wasn't much better, and for Isaac, there was never going to be a way to make things easy."

"If Isaac was everything you say, then I don't see what a problem would have been."

Wilder gave a smile hinting the next thing she said would not be comfortable.

"We're a rural school district, Mr. Malone," she said. "The kids here, they come from poverty that would curl your hair, except you live here, so I'm sure you're all-too familiar with it. And no amount of education or effort will cause some kids to change their minds about things someone has taught them to believe."

I listened to the practiced tone of Wilder's words. She'd made a speech like this before. It rang with familiarity.

"Is Isaac gay?" I said.

"He was. I use the past tense, like it's changed, but I imagine he still is. Unlike a lot of young people, Isaac never tried to hide it. Again, he never tried to be anything other than the person he was. He didn't work to hide being gay, but it never became his defining trait, either. He treated it as fact, along with everything else about him." She spun in her chair and glanced through the office window looking out at the football field, and the running track that encircled it.

Several students did laps around the track. Their strides were long and easy, with no hurry or rush in their movements, enjoying the action of running—if you can enjoy running, that is.

"Did being gay keep him from having friends?" I said.

"Not in the strictest sense. He was intelligent and affable, and those are traits that draw others to you. He made friends, but friends at a distance. There was a smattering of grief from some students—jocks, or the deep holler kids, or the religious ones. When he was named valedictorian, a church protested, held up signs claiming Isaac lived 'a Satanic lifestyle.' A few students joined in with the church. Another time, someone broke into Isaac's locker, filled with warm yogurt, and a note which said something charming like 'bet you can't swallow this.'"

"Pleasant."

"Quite. The harsh truth is, sometimes these kids are animals. I want to believe they can be better, but too often, they can't, and we're trying to make them ready for the world, when in fact the world isn't ready for them. It didn't help who his family is."

I cocked an eyebrow. "Who is his family?"

"You don't know?"

"I wouldn't be asking if I knew already, Dr. Wilder."

"Isaac's a McCoy."

"Yes, and there're more strains of McCoys running through this county than brands of the flu."

"You don't understand what I'm saying. There may be a thousand McCoys in Parker County, but there's only one kind that counts."

And that was when the light of recognition hit me, and I muttered curses under my breath.

"Yes," she said.

She walked me back to her office door.

"Do you have a business card or anything?" she said as I stood at the door. "In case I think of anything, so I can call."

I dug a scrap of paper out of my pocket and scribbled my number. "Feel free to give me a ring if you think of anything."

Wilder smiled. "Certainly."

CHAPTER 8

Woody and I stood behind his house at his shooting range. He popped off shots with a German-made nine millimeter into a silhouette target. Two taps to the head, three to the chest, and one at the crotch to make a point. He emptied the clip, removed his shooting goggles and earplugs, and we walked over to the target. Everything kept in a tight grouping, full of intention. Woody rarely missed what he aimed for.

The shooting range was an open-air setup Woody had built himself behind his farmhouse. The ground was littered with spent cartridges from the endless number of guns he owned. Woody believed in the axiom about a well-armed society being a polite society; with that in mind, Woody was by far the most polite person I'd ever met.

His pack of rescue dogs sat on the back porch, staring through the screen door. Woody and I had enclosed the porch a month earlier, throwing up mesh screening around it because Woody said he had tired of having to share the space with mosquitos the size of ponies. I'd told him everyone liked ponies; he hadn't cared.

"Good shooting there, Tex," I said.

"It'll do." He tore down the target and taped a fresh one onto the hay bales. "Your friend is looking for a McCoy of the 'McCoy' McCoys."

"Looks that way."

"Wouldn't asking you to stab yourself in the neck be an easier way to watch you die?"

"Thank you for that round of optimism."

"False hope has no place if you're dealing with the McCoys. They've been pot farmers in Parker County for longer than anyone can remember, and they're good at it. They've made more money from it than you'll see in a dozen lifetimes; they just opt to appear that they live in squalor."

Back at the firing area, Woody steadied his stance, pushing his feet into the soft soil, drawing his pistol level, closing one eye. While I don't think there's anything particularly romantic in firing a gun—it's all practice, patience and pulling a trigger—Woody had it to a science.

He emptied the clip again. He put the 15 shots where he wanted them to be: five in the head, two in each shoulder, and six in the chest.

Woody lit a cigarette. "Story is that a group of Italian businessman came from Clarksburg to talk to the McCoys—this must have been about 1950—because after Robert Mitchum got busted for marijuana possession, it sounded like maybe the pot thing was going to catch on."

"Italian businessmen?" I said. "So the Mob?"

Woody shook his head. "Certainly not. I'd never make that kind of claim. No, these were just Italian businessmen who maintained an interest in affairs both here and in Sicily. But these businessmen, they saw the McCoys as the perfect stepping stones into the marijuana trade, and they thought they would step in and take over. They sent 10 or 12 guys in to convince the McCoys to work for them. They drove up McCoy Holler with guns and baseball bats at noon. One person drove out of there that night, with the message that the McCoys didn't work for anyone but themselves."

"What happened to the other guys?"

Woody shrugged. "No idea. Rumor was they fed 'em to their hogs. Others said they got buried and turned into fertilizer for the next year's crop."

"Goddamn."

"The McCoys don't play. They get left alone because people know better. No one wants to be the next test of what they're capable of doing."

Woody stepped aside and gestured for me to take my shots. I was shooting a Sig Sauer he had loaned me. Despite years with the state police, and a lifetime in West Virginia, one of the Second Amendment-iest states imaginable, I'm not what you'd call a "gun guy." I was an acceptable shot, could get the job done when need be, but I didn't like to use a gun if I didn't have to. I'd only drawn and fired my service weapon once when I was a state trooper, and that was to stop the guy who'd shotgunned me in the knees three seconds earlier. I had made that shot—and the other 14 in the clip—count.

I moved into the spot, sucked in a deep breath, brought my gun up, took aim. The warm sun bore down on us. A bead of sweat raced its way down my forehead, over my left eyebrow, and dripped behind my shooting glasses, onto my cheek.

I opened fire.

I felt the weight of the weapon with each pull of the trigger. Watched as each shot burrowed itself into the target wall, and each spent shell ejected itself from the pistol and dropped the ground. Held each breath as I took another shot. I kept firing until the weapon's action said the clip was empty.

Woody and I inspected the target. I'd put several shots in the shoulder area, two in what would have been love handles for most folks, and the rest in his general vicinity. It was shooting meant more to annoy someone than to stop them.

Woody heaved a deep sigh. "Goddammit, but you suck something awful, son."

Even I could handle only so much shame and humiliation, so we headed inside to drink coffee. We sat at the kitchen table as the coffee bubbled away in the percolator.

One of Woody's latest acquisitions, something like a mix between a pit bull and a piece of heavy machinery, walked over and pushed his head up underneath my hand. He had an underbite that jutted his lower jaw out a quarter-inch too far, with teeth like a T. Rex and a tongue so long he could lick his eyeballs. He was lean and well-muscled, and his brindle coat glistened in the kitchen light. I rubbed his head, and he made a noise like a car engine in need of carburetor work.

"No offense on this—" I said.

"Which all but guarantees I'm taking offense."

"This guy is ugly even by the standards of the ones you have around here."

Woody smiled. He had a particular smile he reserved for his brand of strays—lopsided and bemused. He never smiled that way because of humans.

"Link might be a special case. He's not quite right, so he's most likely a foster fail."

Woody took in strays, intent on rehabbing them and sending them to rescue groups that found them new homes. Sometimes things didn't work out, those times based around Woody getting too attached, and they ended up staying, hence the "foster fail."

I kept scratching and rubbing at Link's head. His skull felt weird, as rough and un-contoured as a country road. He closed his eyes, and something close to a smile threatened to curl up from the corners of his lips. I pulled my hand back, and his eyes popped open and the noise of pleasure rumbling from within him turned into a growl. I went back to rubbing his head.

The coffee finished, and Woody poured it and set the cups on the table. He tapped Link on the back. Link's head snapped around to stare at Woody. Woody said something in German and pointed toward the living room. I think Link might have sighed before he dropped his head and trotted out to join the rest of the dogs.

I dumped milk and sugar into the coffee and took a sip.

Woody's coffee was the consistency of hot mud, but it was strong and guaranteed to keep you awake, likely for days on end. He took his black. Showoff.

"The McCoys are nasty souls," Woody said, drinking coffee from a mug with a picture of a cat swinging from a bar and the caption "Hang In There!" "Where the National Brotherhood only had ignorance and fear as a common bond, the McCoys have ignorance, fear, shared bloodlines, and a marijuana business worth millions."

"The likelihood of them helping us find Isaac is slim, is what you're saying."

"It is. They've got an Old Testament worldview about things, and a chunk of that keeps them separate from the world."

"What about the fact about being Isaac's gay, and he never hid the fact?"

"That might not matter to Tennis McCoy. The overriding factor for him is family, no matter who they opt to bed down with at night. You got their last name, they will fight for you to the end."

"Tennis McCoy is the family patriarch, I am to presume?"

"Presume away. He was a kid when the Italian businessmen came by, and he's been running the show for decades now. He is an old man in a business that doesn't encourage longevity. You've got to ask yourself what's he done to make sure he lives so long. The correct answer is 'whatever the fuck it takes.' Then ask yourself if this is shit you want to dive into."

"You're putting out a lot of questions for me to be asking myself, and you're well aware I'm not introspective in the least."

"You're a shallow puddle on a sunny day."

"Such a sweetheart you are. I figure I've got a few days off. I don't guess there's nothing good on TV until the new season of *Game of Thrones* starts. I say to myself, 'Meh, why not?'"

"As long as your reasoning is sound. This friend of yours, Pete, he's a good guy?"

"Wasn't like we were best friends, but he was always steady, always honest."

"And he's a private investigator now."

"Got business cards and everything."

"If he's got business cards then yeah, obviously his shit is legit. What are you getting out of this, he gets Isaac McCoy back?"

"Part of his fee, which I'll split with you if you'll help." I leaned back in my chair and looked through the doorway into the living room. Six or seven dogs were scattered throughout, stretched out on the floor or sleeping on the couch. "It'd buy you some dog food. Last you through a week or two, at least."

"At least." Woody finished his coffee and poured himself another cup. "I'm sure I'll regret this. I might regret it already."

"What's life without a little regret?" I said.

"A not-unpleasant idea," he said.

CHAPTER 9

Pete answered the door to his room when I knocked. He smiled, shook Woody's hand and introduced himself, and waved us inside.

The TV glowed with life, turned to one of those crime shows where they're always looking at stuff underneath a black light and sending samples to the guys in the lab. Pete wore what he'd been wearing earlier in the day, but he looked worse in it. Tired, as if the day had dragged down on him.

Pete went to the mini-fridge and got himself a beer. He looked back at us and said, "I know what your answer's gonna be, Henry, but what about you, Woody? Get you one?"

We had taken the chairs next to the window. "My answer's gonna be the same as Henry's," Woody said.

Pete shook his head. "Damn, but you boys are killing me here." He twisted the cap off the bottle and took a swallow and sat on the edge of the bed. "So what d'you find out?"

I leaned forward and propped my elbows up on my knees and tried to look thoughtful. "That things are more complicated than you thought."

I explained to Pete about talking to Dr. Wilder, and the McCoys. He drank his beer as I talked, having me stop at one point so he could grab another. His expression didn't change much, but something shifted in his eyes. The look was one that said he wasn't sure when he'd been lied to, but someone hadn't been telling him the truth.

I said, "Dealing with the McCoys, if it's where this goes, might be a situation we don't want."

Pete stared down at his beer. "There's not much of a choice. I have to find this guy."

Woody said, "The McCoys are bad mamma-jammers, Pete. If this guy you're looking for, if he is at the McCoys' farm, the family's won't just tell us. He's hiding for a reason. The question then becomes if you think they came and got him, or he's here of his own free will?"

"No idea," Pete said. "There's no reason he would up and run. This guy's personal life was clean. Damn near sparkled."

"The personal life was all a lie, Pete," I said. "He tried to become someone else for a reason."

Pete's hand drifted back to the wedding band. He wasn't looking at us anymore. "Not all of it." His voice sounded thick and wet. "It all can't be a lie."

I glanced over at Woody, raised my eyebrows. He gave me a small nod.

"Pete," I said, "you need to be honest with Woody and me if you want us to help you."

"What are you talking about?" Pete said.

"I mean about you and Isaac McCoy. If you're going into this thing with a vested interest that could put us at risk, you need to tell us now."

Pete trembled as tears ran down his face. The trembling grew into shaking, and the tears flowed faster and freer, and his big walrus-y face turned red and blotchy, and he buried it in his huge hands as his body vibrated, and from behind those hands came a mournful noise, this pained groaning as this big man broke down in the rawest, most human way possible.

Woody pulled out a bunch of tissues from the dispenser at the bathroom sink and set them next to Pete, then took his own seat again. We sat without saying a word for a brief eternity. I heard Pete pull a huge breath in, and he brought his hands down and looked up at us with swollen eyes and little bubbles of snot popping out of his nose. He took a handful of the tissues and wiped at his eyes and blew his nose a few times. He trudged to the sink and ran water over his face and toweled off and sat back down on the bed.

"I'm sorry," he said. "I wasn't sure what you'd say."

"There's nothing to say. But this isn't strictly a business transaction anymore, so how we handle everything involving the McCoys becomes affected by how you deal with the situation."

He pushed tears away from the corners of his eyes. "What was the big tip?"

"There was nothing in the way you talked about this that felt like it was only business," Woody said.

"Plus, you kept messing with your ring," I said. "The photo you showed me this afternoon, there was an arm around Isaac, and the hand, it had the same ring as what you're wearing. The hand in the photo looked the same as your hand. You've got rather distinctive mitts, Pete."

"Yeah, I suppose I knew it'd come to this. I...I would have told you. I wasn't sure when the right time was."

"At the beginning would have been good, but now works, too."

Pete sucked back snot. "Isaac and I, we drove up to Vermont. This was back before the Supreme Court and everything, and only a few places were doing it. Our friends, other couples, they were putting rings on and doing this big show about the whole thing, and me, I didn't get it. The whole gay marriage thing, that kind of fight was never for me; I wanted to be quiet and left alone. But Isaac, he kept on and on about how he wanted to get married. He said it was important. Plus, he said he wanted me to make an honest man out of him finally."

Pete looked down at the ring. "I did my full thirty with the state police and spent the whole time hiding who I was," Pete said. "How the fuck would I ever tell those guys something like that?"

"People are more accepting than they used to be," I said.

"It's different when you wear a uniform. Different when you spend hour after hour in a patrol car with someone. Everything's attitude, about being a bigger bad ass than the other guy, and none of that mattered even if I could have kicked everyone's ass, because I would still be a faggot to them."

Pete drank some of his beer. He still looked like a tomato with a crew cut, but the redness of his face was fading down to skin tone. "There're sodas in the refrigerator, too. I don't want you to think I'm a drunk or something. I guess I've been drinking more since—"

I leaned forward, elbows on knees, hands together, thoughtful expression on my face. Someone might have mistaken me for someone who had a clue what the hell he was doing. "I need you to tell us what's going on with you and Isaac. Not just the basics, either. The whole thing."

CHAPTER 10

"We've been together about two years," Pete said. "Isaac's younger, obviously. I don't have a thing for younger guys, anything like that. I'm not sure what I was thinking, getting involved with someone his age. Sometimes I feel like one of those sad old queers who thinks if he dates enough young guys, he'll never grow old. But you hit my age, there's not much in the dating pool worth shaving your balls for, so to speak, and Isaac all but came looking for me."

Pete's fresh beer sat untouched on the nightstand. He folded his hands onto his lap. As he talked, he almost got younger before my eyes. We're talking Pete, though, so it was just degrees of Wilford Brimley, but still, it happened.

"I drove up to Pittsburgh for a wine and jazz festival; the music was good, the wine less so," he said. "My friends rambled on about shit I didn't care about, and Isaac must have seen the boredom on my face, because he appeared from nowhere and struck up a conversation with me. Once my friends left and people cleared out, he and I got coffee and talked the rest of the night, and before I had blinked, it was morning.

"Isaac's too pretty to be straight, but I never connected in my head him being interested in me. All we did that night was talk. He was funny, and smart, and interesting. He talked about what he was doing with Cashbyte, and I didn't understand, but I didn't care, either. He asked me about being a cop, and when the sun rose, he kissed me and slipped me his business card and told me to call him. I fought it as long as I could. I put his card on my refrigerator and I stared at it for three days, every time I poured a glass of orange juice, or got a beer, that card stared back at me, demanding when I planned to sack up and do this thing. When I did, Isaac said, 'What the fuck took you so long?'"

"How had he been acting the past few weeks?" I said. "Any weird behaviors? Anything different?"

Pete nodded. "Everything started about a month ago, when he called me from work one day. He and his partners rent office space at a business park, and Isaac, he said he thought someone followed him as he drove in that morning. I asked him why, and he said he recognized this car, a Ford or a Chevy, he wasn't sure of which, but he was sure it followed him from the house to the office. I told him he was imagining things, cars all look alike these days, and I guess he was okay for a while, but then the next day he said the same thing happened.

"So one day, after he left for work, I waited a minute or two, and then I followed him, and I noticed another car—a Ford—following him. The drive isn't a straight line, and if you're going from one to another, you're doing so for a reason. Then I tested the idea again, and this time, the car bailed out after a point, and another car picked up for a while, but then the first car showed back up, and it finished the drive all the way to Isaac's office."

"This sounds like professionals," Woody said. "Tails with a team. They knew what they were doing."

"Anything else weird?" I said.

Pete said, "The last two weeks, I'd catch him on the phone, talking, but when I asked him who he was talking to, he got quiet, wouldn't say anything. He'd say it was Patrick or Vikram and then he'd try to steer into something else. He made it clear he didn't want to talk about the phone calls, and I'm not proud of this, but I went to check his call history on his phone when he was in the shower one day, and he had a lock on his phone.

It was one where he needed to swipe a fingerprint across a scanner on the back, and I couldn't open it. He'd never had a lock before, and we had always talked about never having secrets."

"Did you look at his cell phone bill?"

"No. He keeps everything all online—he's so big on everything being paperless—and I didn't know the password. I never needed to because I always trusted him." His shoulder slumped forward, and it seemed something inside him had broken and he might collapse in on himself. "I'm sorry. I'm an old man, and I've never let myself be in this a situation, and now I'm clueless about what to do."

Woody sat down next to Pete on the bed and put his hand on Pete's shoulder. "We'll help you find him."

I smiled and said to Woody, "Can we step outside for a few?"

We walked to the other side of the motel parking lot.

"No way," I said. "This is a terrible idea. This is personal with Pete, and it will be a disaster. That's a sensation in my fucking bones."

Woody lit a cigarette. "He's your friend. You dragged me into this when you thought it was only money. Now you find out he's got a personal involvement, you're ready to cut and run?"

I gestured for Woody to hand me the pack and his lighter. He slapped them into my hand and said, "You should try buying your own for once."

"Why, when my friends keep letting me bum theirs?" I said. The first drag was relaxing and wonderful. I pushed the smoke out of my lungs. "When it was only about us making money, yes, I was good with working, because we weren't risking our lives for the love of someone's life."

"So you're not okay with this being personal for Isaac. You'd rather he maybe loses this person he loves."

I sucked in more smoke and exhaled. "When you put things like that, I sound like an asshole."

"There's a reason you sound like an asshole, and that would be because you're an asshole."

I scratched at my face. "I'm wondering how far Pete's willing to go, and will it be so far we end up getting killed." I held up my left hand. "Perhaps you remember having to stitch my hand back up. What's to say the McCoys don't have the same tendencies, and they lop off our thumbs? That'll put a huge crimp in my Xbox habit."

"Wouldn't happen. The McCoys, they'd cut your balls off."

"Not making me feel better."

"Not trying to. What I am saying is your friend is hurting in there, and what a sad fucking affair how I've known him 10 minutes and I'll go to bat for him, and you won't."

Goddammit, but I hated Woody sometimes. I hated when he was right. I hated he was so fucking loyal. He could almost put his dogs to shame that way.

I finished my cigarette. "Let's tell him we'll do it."

"Good lad."

"Fuck you." I said and walked back toward Pete's room. I had my hand raised to knock on the door when I stopped and looked at Woody behind me. "You understand we won't get paid for this now? He'd have had to have pulled cash from his own pocket and neither one of us can take the money now."

"Was never doing this for money anyway," Woody said.

"Then why the hell were you doing it?"

Woody jerked his chin toward the room. "Knock on the door," he said.

CHAPTER 11

Woody and I made the eight a.m. St. Anthony's meeting the next morning. I didn't have much to say, and Woody said he was grateful to be sober and passed on to the next guy.

I was sulking still from the night prior, less because Woody had won the argument and more because I had been open to throwing Pete and his problems under the bus. I didn't like what it said about me, my selfishness, or my lack of willingness to risk.

This could be simple. Perhaps we would find Isaac, and he and Pete would go home, and no one would get shot, for once. But I knew there was no way it would be simple. Nothing was simple for me these days.

We picked Pete up and swung over to Tudor's for breakfast. Pete had eggs, biscuits, hash browns and bacon, while Woody had biscuits and gravy and told them to keep them coming until he said stop. I had an egg and cheese biscuit I picked at without doing much damage to.

A waitress came by and refilled our coffee cups. Woody sipped on his. To Pete, he said, "So Isaac never talked to you about his family?"

"Never," Pete said. "Early on he told me both of his parents died while he was in college. He didn't act like he had a lot of pleasant memories about anyone."

"That part could well be true. There's not a reputation for

the McCoys being overrun with the milk of human kindness." Woody looked at Pete. "Isaac may have tried to run away from his family, from the history of his family and make himself out into someone new, but everyone has long shadows you can't avoid because you want to."

"Meaning what?" Pete had his silverware in his hands, but he'd stopped eating, and held his knife and fork at the ready, his knuckles draining of blood as he pressed his fingers tighter into his palms.

"Meaning you may not care much for the person we end up finding. He's not necessarily going to be the same person you're in love with."

"I know who he is."

"What if he won't go back?" I said.

Pete looked at me as if I'd asked about swimming naked in a pool of marinara sauce. "Why wouldn't he?"

"Because if he's hiding for a reason, it denotes he doesn't want found, and he might not want to come home."

"Let me talk to him. Let me get the answers," Pete said. "Whatever they are, I'll take them, and move on from there."

He said the words. Nothing implied he meant a single one.

Woody pushed a chunk of biscuit around his plate with the end of his fork, sopping up as much gravy as possible.

The waitress came by with a fresh plate for him.

"What's this make you?" I said. "Your third?"

"Fourth."

"Have you no respect for your arteries?"

"None." To Pete, Woody said, "Has Isaac been getting threats?"

"He never said anything to me if he was."

"What about people calling you guys out, saying things?" I said.

"What kind of things?"

I blew out a huge sigh. "Must we go there?"

"Yes, we must."

I leaned in across the table and dropped my voice. "Anything homophobic," I said. "Anything derogatory."

Pete sipped his coffee. "Are you asking if someone called him or me a queer, a faggot, a fairy, an ass bandit, cock knockers, shit stabbers, rump rangers, ass munchers, pillow biters, cock gobblers, fudge packers, size queens, a rear admiral—" He took a breath. "I can keep this up all day."

"Please don't. It makes me despair for the species too much."

"People put forth a lot of work to be hateful," Woody said.

"People find what they're good at and work towards a goal," Pete said. "And no one's said anything to Isaac or I that either one don't already hear. It's the same shit any two men would get anywhere, especially in West Virginia, but we let things slide and focus on what's important."

"Why weren't you going to tell me the truth to start off?" I said.

"Because back when you were on patrol, you said a lot of the same garbage others guys said, calling people 'fags,' making jokes and acting like it wasn't nothing. You said shit to guys in uniform I knew were so far back in the closet they could see Narnia."

"Like who?"

"Frank Waters. Younger than me," Pete said. "Gray hair, mustache. Detective."

An image of Frank's face hit me. "He was gay?"

"Been partnered with the same guy 22 years. I went to their anniversary party last month."

"I used to play basketball with him. We were on an intramural league." A beat. "We used to shower together after games."

"That sounds way more intimate than I expected," Woody said.

"Yeah," Pete said. "He said good things about you."

"Was he checking out my dick?"

"No, you homophobic asshole, he wasn't. He said you had a strong outside shot. But do you see how you responded?

Reactions like yours are why telling the truth is difficult." He looked at Woody. "I need help from someone who isn't an idiot. What do we do now?"

Woody finished the last bite of biscuit and gravy and waved toward the waitress. She brought him another full plate. He considered it for a moment, took a bite.

"We go to the McCoy family and meet with the paterfamilias."

CHAPTER 12

Maggie called as we walked out of Tudor's. I told Pete and Woody I'd catch up, and I waited until I had some distance between us before I answered.

I'd been dodging her. Not fair, or mature, but I'd never been accused of being either, least of all by her.

I sucked in some air and said, "Hey."

"You should try answering phone calls sometime," she said. "I left voice mails. You never call me back."

"I've been getting people trying to sell me aluminum siding. You're not going to try to sell me siding, are you?"

"No, Henry." Her tone was as flat as 50 miles of Kansas highway.

There was a cacophony of voices in the background, blurring and blending together with keyboard clattering. Someone yelled about finishing a rewrite. Someone else said the city planner was on line four.

I'd struggled to not take Maggie's move to Philadelphia as a personal affront, placing even more miles between us. I suppose the metaphorical emotional distance between us was the larger of those gaps. That said, I wasn't one big on metaphor. None of that made this hurt any less.

"You're at work," I said.

"Ever the observant soul. I'm waiting on the governor's office to call."

"I'm glad you could find time to squeeze me in."

"I call you when it's convenient for me, not the other way around. If you want to talk, try calling me when it's good for you, instead of me calling when I'm neck deep on deadline."

"It's a new world, Mags; don't you operate on a 24-hour news cycle now?"

"I do, but I'm out of town for a few days. I won't be able to talk until I'm back."

"Where you headed?"

"Somewhere."

"Somewhere's nice this time of year. The skiing is good. Are you going Somewhere with anyone in particular?"

"Yes."

That one word, it carried the weight of a trainload of elephants.

I wanted to ask. I knew the answer already—not a name, only that he wasn't me—but I wanted her to say it. But I didn't, either, because there was no going back from there.

"Henry," she said.

Even over the din of noise swirling around her, I heard my breathing, the sound of air cycling through the phone's microphone and back into my ear. The sound was strained and harsh. I couldn't even register the sound emanated from me. It was just another noise, another distraction.

"Henry," she said again.

I swallowed hard. "I'm here."

"I need you to sign the papers, honey." The even, emotionless tone was gone. Her voice was soft, the way she would sound when we would wake up, sometimes hung over, sometimes not, and she'd roll over and look at me with a smile framed by masses of dark hair thrown around her face. Her voice was smooth and gentle those mornings, and she would reach over and place her hands across my face, the brush of her soft skin against my stubbled cheeks, and her smile would grow even brighter, her blue eyes shining in the morning light and the scent of her lotion lingering on her hands.

It all hit me, in a second, in a word.

Honey.

"I know," I said.

"Is there a reason you're not signing them?"

"I think Izzy ate them."

"Izzy is the dog, right?"

Maggie had never met Izzy. Had never seen the trailer where I lived now. Had seen nothing of whatever kind of life I was making for myself. It was just as well. I wouldn't want her to be envious of my rock star existence.

"Should the lawyer send new copies?" she said.

"Yeah. Have him do that," I said.

"I will. First thing tomorrow. Certified mail."

"I'll be waiting with bated breath."

"Try gum. Or mouth rinse. Gotta go. The governor's office is calling."

I didn't want the conversation to end. Keep talking, Maggie, just a little while longer. I didn't care what she said, as long as her voice stayed on the line. More than the smell of her perfume, almost more the feel of her body or the touch of her hair, I missed her voice. There was comfort and promise and hope in her voice, and I needed to hold on to the sound, the possibility of her, a while longer.

"Have a good rest of the day," I said.

"You too," she said, as the line went dead.

I shoved the phone in my back pocket and headed toward Woody's truck. He leaned against the driver's side door, smoking.

"You've looked happier," he said.

"Where's Pete?"

"Ran back inside to the little boys' room, to drain the main vein. Was that Maggie?"

Before I could answer, Pete came through Tudor's exit about the same moment, wiping his hands on his pants.

"Too much goddamn coffee," he said, laughing. "Whew."

Woody took a drag of his cigarette. "You need a minute?"

I shook my head. “I’m solid.”

Woody put out his cigarette. “Then let’s rock ’n’ roll, rock ’n’ rollers.”

CHAPTER 13

I'd gone out west with Maggie years prior, to Oregon to visit her family, and I remembered staring at those mountains—real mountains that stretched until they threatened to pierce the blue of the sky. We climbed Mount Hood while we visited, brought a sleeping bag with us, made love amid the wildness, and she told me how Mount Hood was an active volcano, though unlikely to erupt. No matter; you still had a city of more than a half-million living in the shadow of a volcano.

"It's something to keep your karma level," she said, snuggling closer.

West Virginia mountains are less than that, yet somehow more. They're tree-encrusted nubs of rock rolling throughout the state, screwing up the topography in every direction. There's so little flat land in West Virginia, you ponder if it was perseverance, stupidity, or both that led people to stay here. But we cling with pride to those mountains. We call ourselves Mountaineers, and we say so in the state motto, how Mountaineers are always free.

A few years ago, the boss of an out-of-state coal company that's one of the state's de facto absentee landlords, he said if we let him do mountaintop removal for his mining operations, he'd give West Virginia all the flat land we could ever want. That had cracked up the audience, a bunch of expensive suits and politicians who may as well as had their hats in hand, asking for spare change. It was where I felt Mountaineers maybe weren't so much free as just open to the best offer.

Woody drove his cherry red 1965 Ford pickup up the winding lane-and-a-half of rutted blacktop that made up Muddy Creek Road. On the left, a narrow stream the color of coffee with cream gushed by us. Kids playing in the water, splashing, pulling up rocks and examining underneath them with fierce interest, as if they would discover the secrets to the universe.

This was the classic definition of a "holler," which should never be confused with a "hollow'; that sounds too proper and possibly New England-ish, and is therefore surely gay. No, a holler is some sliver of space between two mountains with just enough open air to let someone convince themselves that slapping down a road and building homes here is a good idea.

A holler is where the cycle spins endlessly. Families are born and raised and start afresh each generation, never leaving one another's watchful eyes. Instead, you find someone to breed that next generation with, buy yourself a doublewide within spitting distance of the people who share your last name, and rest secure in the knowledge that whatever was good enough for them is still good enough for you.

We kept driving, and the road thinned until the edges of the truck tires almost hung over the sides, and trailers grew more raggedy, sadder and sparer, older and more weathered, until they seemed unfit for human use. Children rode bicycles in circles around front yards that were nothing but weeds and patches of dirt. A roar came from the hillsides, the sounds of four-wheelers whipping through the terrain. We passed a trailer with an old-school satellite dish on the hillside behind it, a monstrosity fit for monitoring for alien communication.

We drove in silence. Pete sat on the passenger side, his arm half-hanging out of the window. I was squeezed between them, my knees straddling the gearshift. Woody kept the truck in second, the transmission whining like a whipped puppy. We made new turns, and the blacktop ended, and we cranked up a gravel road to McCoy Holler. We knocked around inside the truck cab like marbles in a 55-gallon drum for a half-mile before we approached a metal gate blocking the road. The gate was chained and locked, and on either side, barbed wire fencing ran out into the distance.

Woody braked the truck to a stop and shut the engine off. "This is where we walk," he said.

Pete looked at him like he was crazy. I recognized the face because I gave Woody the same expression more often than there are sunsets. "Are you kidding me?" he said.

"I am not," Woody said.

Pete climbed out of the truck cab. He shielded his eyes with the flat of his hand, surveying the dirt road. "What the fuck am I getting into?"

Woody got out on the driver's side. "There's the same question we should all ask when we fall in love."

We climbed underneath the gate and started walking. Woody packed a nine millimeter, and Pete and I both had forty-fives. We kept them shoved in the back of our jeans and our shirt tails pulled out over top. It wasn't like we could hide them, and anyone with a brain would notice if they looked, but we had decided going out to see the McCoys unarmed was an invitation to a shallow grave.

We walked for what seemed forever. To someone without an artificial knee, it may have been so bad, but for me, on uneven road, with the sun beating down on me, the whole thing felt like a death march. A murder of crows circled overhead, dancing through the air. I wondered what possessed the person who determined how things got named to make "murder" the collective noun for crows. Did that say something about the person who made those kinds of decisions, or something about crows themselves?

I bet you've thought weird shit, too, when you were walking

and bored and hot. Don't judge me.

The only sound was our footsteps crunching against gravel as the road curved and flattened out, and a small house appeared in the opening expanse about a quarter-mile ahead, and further in the distance rested a large weathered barn.

My knee ached, the throbbing coursing through my thigh and stretching into my hips. I wiped sweat off my brow and heaved a breath that doubled as a sigh of relief. I wasn't happy to arrive to the McCoys' property as much as I didn't want to walk anymore.

"How long do you think it'll be before they notice us coming?" I said.

A rifle shot rang out. Dust spat up from the road three feet in front of us.

"I'd say about now," Woody said.

Pete reached back for his gun.

"Don't," Woody said. "If they'd wanted to hit us, we'd be sucking air through holes in our necks. That was a warning shot, to let us know they know we're here."

"I'd call it effective," I said.

"No one's accusing them of subtlety."

A four-wheeler growled to life and sped out toward us. The driver was youngish, teens, no helmet, ruddy faced with scraggly patches of hair growing without caution or planning across his face. A gimme John Deere cap was shoved backwards on his head. He was wiry, wearing a filthy T-shirt and camo cargo pants and work boots.

The kid hit the brakes on the four-wheeler hard and did a fancy little spin that threw dirt and rocks on us. Dust gathered in my mouth, and I shut my eyes as gravel bounced off me. Once I figured the air was clear, I opened my eyes and saw the little prick staring at us with a shit-eating grin full of satisfaction. He had a pistol in a holster, and a .30-06 strapped across his back. He shifted his expression to disdain, like we were coming to fornicate with the livestock, and he'd had to look up what "fornicate" meant. He spit on the ground.

"The fuck you want?" he said.

I raised my hands into clear view and took a slight step forward. He shifted a hand from the handlebars to the .45.

"We're trying to find Isaac McCoy," I said.

The kid's eyes moved from one side to the other.

"You cocksuckers cops?"

"We are not," I said. "But Isaac's missing, and we hoped he's spoken to his family."

The kid pulled his hat off, and a bushel of wiry brown hair sprang to life. He scratched at his scalp and pushed the mop of hair back underneath the cap and reached into a cargo pants pocket for a walkie-talkie.

"Hey, Greg," he said into the device.

The walkie-talkie crackled, and a voice said, "Yeah, Jed."

"Those fuck-nuggets you popped a shot at? They're looking for Isaac."

"Do tell." Laughter erupted from the device. "They faggots too?"

The kid snorted a laugh. "They look like it. Let Grandpa know."

More laughter from the walkie-talkie. "Hold up." The walkie-talkie went dead. The kid set the device down on the four-wheeler's gas tank and put his hand back on the pistol in the holster. He slit his eyes narrow and said, "You suck dick like Isaac?"

"Only your mother's," I said.

The kid didn't smile. Behind me, Woody groaned.

The voice came from the walkie-talkie again. "Grandpa said to bring 'em on up to the house."

"Can do," the kid. To us, he said, "You sack-suckers think you can make the walk to the house without stopping to ass-fuck each other?"

"You think your parents ever have days where they'd wished your mother had just wiped you off her chin instead?" I said.

He cranked up the four-wheeler and spun it again, covering us in another layer of dirt and rocks before he yelled, “Follow me!” and hauled ass back up the road.

I turned to Woody. “I bet they don’t offer us lunch.”

CHAPTER 14

"Pissing them off won't help this situation," Woody said as we got closer to the house.

"Are you saying my approach lacks tact?" I said.

"I'm saying you've got the dial cranked up well past the 'asshole" setting you operate at on a good day."

The main McCoy property was a small farmhouse that looked like dried dogshit. Rust encrusted the tin roof, the paint peeled off in strips, and the lawn was deader than a trust in politics. A Dagwood sandwich mutt laid in a wide dusty spot, its white face flat against the ground. An eye flickered open, and he evaluated us as a threat or not, decided we weren't, and went back to dreaming the dreams of old dogs.

A screen door banged open and a man somewhere in his 70s stepped out. He was as small and compact as a dwarf star. He had probably been in decent shape 10 or 12 presidential administrations ago, constructed like a welterweight, but time took care of that, turning muscle slack and leaving skin to hang without care from his body. He wore a white tank top, Wranglers cinched by a belt with a buckle large enough to be a hubcap, silver-tipped cowboy boots, and a cowboy hat with a raven feather sticking out from the band, glistening in the sun. He had on mirrored sunglasses and rings on each finger.

The kid who'd been on the four-wheeler came out of the house behind the old man. Now he had the shotgun in his hands, and an angry expression that said we were not going to be invited to lunch. He kept two respectful steps behind.

The old man said, "Which one of you is Pete?"

Pete nodded. "That'd be me."

The old man stepped over to Pete and extended his hand. "My son, he talks real highly of you."

Pete folded his own hand into the old man's. A smile broke out on the old man's face. It activated every wrinkle, crinkle and age line he had, and years piled on him like someone had poured them from a cement mixer.

The kid cleared his throat. The old man looked back at him and shook his head.

"Overlook my grandson," the old man said. "He's been to church, getting religion, and he don't approve much of Isaac's life." To the kid, he said, "Go on back inside, Jed."

The kid curled his face up. "But Grandpa—"

"Don't argue with me," the old man said.

The kid nodded and mumbled something and spat hard in our direction, the glob of spit arcing well but dropping off early and landing a few feet shy of us, before walking back inside.

"Need to have him checked for dehydration, he keeps spitting like that," I said.

"Children, they always think they got all the answers?" Tennis McCoy said. "All their life is waiting for old guys like me to die so they move up and be next in line for whatever it is they're waiting on." He looked at Woody and me. "And who are you?"

"I'm Henry Malone, and this is my friend Woody. We're friends of Pete."

The old man took off his sunglasses. His eyes were small and set deep into his face. "Tennis McCoy, Isaac's father." He gestured toward Woody and me. "When you say you're 'friends,' you mean like Isaac and Pete?"

"No. Pete and I used to be state troopers together."

"You told my grandson you weren't cops."

"We're not. We used to be cops. Pete's retired, and I'm no

longer on the force." I suppose life's all about the verb tense.

The old man walked towards Pete and threw his arms around him. Pete stood for a moment, unsure what to do, before pulling his arms loose and returning the embrace.

The old man let cranked his head upward toward Pete. "Isaac loves you."

Pete flickered a smile. "Thank you. Isaac doesn't talk about his family much."

"I imagine he don't. I begrudge no man for following his own path."

"Have you talked to Isaac?" I said. "Heard anything from him the past few days?"

"Can't say I have," McCoy said. "Like I said, Isaac's very much his own person. His computer stuff, those are things way outside anything we worry about. I guess some younger folks, they might know about such things, but me, I'm more about good earth and what grows from it."

"What about where he may have gone?" I said.

"No idea. Isaac's from here, but he's not really 'of here.' He's his own soul. You aren't ignorant about what we do, and that wasn't what Isaac wanted, so he found his own path."

"Any chance we can come inside, look at Isaac's things, see if we can find something?"

McCoy smiled. "Isaac been gone from here a lot of years now. Doubtful anything he's got here from his past would help tell about his now. Besides, we're private people, out of need and necessity as much as just who we are. The fact is, you've gotten this far and we haven't shot you says something." To Pete, he said, "Life's not about easy answers."

"No, sir, it's not."

"And Isaac, he's a bird that might not want caged. I know this has to be hurting you."

Pete nodded and bit on his bottom lip and looked at the ground.

McCoy said he'd be back and headed back into the house.

Woody said, "Man's lying through his teeth. He knows something. He's not even asking about what happened to Isaac. You got any thoughts on what to do next?"

Through a second-story window, the spitting grandson stared at us. A figure had taken a post next to him, another boy about the same age, this one holding a rifle. My eyes moved to other windows and saw other people, also with guns and also with expressions that showed they wouldn't object to shooting someone.

"I suppose there's a reason they didn't check us for weapons," I said.

Woody nodded. "Sometimes it's better to get away, to live to fight another day."

McCoy walked out about that time, holding a small gym bag. He handed the bag to Pete.

"This won't take away the hurt, but maybe it'll help a little," McCoy said. "You go on, have yourself a good life. You move on, build from whatever you got."

Pete opened the bag and looked inside. He shut the bag and stuck it back out toward McCoy. "I can't take this," he said.

McCoy pushed back the brim of his hat. "It's poor manners to refuse a man's generosity. What's there is yours now, so keep it. But now I'm gonna need you folks to roll on back to your vehicle. There's work to tend to today."

What about your son?" I said. "Aren't you the least bit curious where he's at?"

McCoy put the hat back on, adjusted it until shade covered his face. "My son's an adult, capable of taking care of himself. Wherever he is, he's fine, I'm sure. I can't do much beyond that. Now, I've already asked you to leave once. Please don't make me ask twice."

He headed back inside the house. The spitting grandson opened his window from the second floor and aimed his weapon in our direction, as did the other kid with him. Like dominoes tumbling, windows opened and guns pointed at us.

"I think there's our cue to go," Woody said.

CHAPTER 15

We got back to Woody's pickup without having much to say. Pete trudged behind like he was dragging a weight, the gym bag bouncing against his thigh. Once we were in the truck cab, engine running and driving away from the McCoys, my curiosity got the best of me, and I said, "Christ, but let me see what's in the bag."

Pete threw the bag on my lap. A stack of hundred-dollar bills jumped out. Inside the bag were a bunch of its relatives. More hundreds, banded together. I flipped through them, counted, did the math in my head. "The old bastard gave Pete a hundred grand."

"He paid me off like I was a whore," Pete said.

"No offense to you, Pete, but no whore that looked like you would make a hundred grand."

Pete turned his attention out the window. "I'll take half. You can have the rest."

I cocked an eyebrow. "Excuse me?"

"I'll take it, do something with it. Fuck if I have an idea what. You put yourself in harm's way for my sake. It's the least I can do."

Woody rolled down a window and lit a cigarette, blowing the smoke out and letting it trail behind us. "You should wait and let's see if we can figure out what to do next about finding Isaac. I presume you're not giving up."

"His family, they have an inkling where he is, don't they?" Pete said.

"Possibly," Woody said. "I don't believe for a moment the old man doesn't care where his son is. A family like that, there're few moves made that the rest don't know about."

"Tennis was awfully Zen about his son being gay," I said.

"Tennis McCoy has repopulated so many times, one son opting out of the game won't make a dent in the passing of the family lineage," Woody said. "He imagines he's got some bullshit Native American bent, so he looks at Isaac as being 'two spirited.' It's what some tribes used to call those who didn't follow the usual gender route and would dress as braves or squaws instead."

"Isn't 'braves' or 'squaws' brushing with a rather big brush?" I said. "They all didn't say that."

"Are you going to give me grief about this? You know the point I was trying to make. What I'm saying is—"

Pete sighed. "Jesus, but you two should just fuck and get it over with."

Woody laughed. "Not even with someone else's dick."

I held my hand to my chest as if clutching pearls. "That's hurtful."

"The truth is often a hurtful thing."

We dropped Pete off at the motel and drove to Woody's farm. The yapping multitude of dogs greeted us as we walked inside and headed into the kitchen. Woody went to cooking a pot of coffee.

"I was expecting a lot more nightmare out of Tennis McCoy and his kin," I said.

"Don't kid yourself," he said. "Man can act like he's smoking the product, but I wouldn't trust Tennis any farther than I could throw him."

"He's a small guy. Work a good spin on him, you could chuck him a respectable distance, if you threw him Olympic hammer-style."

Some dogs wandered in and gathered around Woody as he made coffee. He moved around them with practiced ease, as if the process were a dance—Fred Astaire if Ginger Rogers had been a pack of strays.

"How do you end up attracting every needy and attention-starved creature in four counties?" I said.

"A question I've pondered since we met."

From the stove, the percolator gurgled and popped.

The coffee finished, and Woody filled our mugs. He only poured mine two-thirds full, and I evened it out with milk and sugar. The first sip was the hardest, a thick, almost sludgy thing that takes a moment to appreciate, and by "appreciate," I mean "pray to God it doesn't kill you." Woody's coffee was the stuff of 1950s horror pictures, a concoction developing sentience and bound to take over the world. You couldn't stop it; you could only hope to contain it, one cup at a time.

"Not letting us in, and being adamant about it, that seemed suspicious," I said.

"He wasn't expecting company. And the man is a pot farmer. You don't just let strangers into your house, you've got illegal activity going on."

"Didn't stop him from dropping a hundred large on Pete like it was pocket change. Which reminds me: what the hell were you thinking, telling Pete to keep the money?"

"We've not done anything to deserve Pete giving us that much money. Driving him out to the McCoy place doesn't equate him shelling out fifty thousand dollars for gas money."

I sipped at the coffee. It didn't get better with time. If anything, it only got angrier and more bitter sitting in the cup, as if plotting revenge for perceived wrongs.

"Should we go back?" I said.

"Maybe. Not yet, though. Doubtful McCoy would change his story."

"There's more going on here, though. Is it possible the Feds were following Isaac?"

"It sure as hell sounds like the way they operate. The question then becomes, what do the Feds want with Isaac?"

"There's this weird anonymous, untraceable currency he's developed, and then there's the fact his old man's a drug kingpin. Either one would be a good starting point for a Feeb with a little curiosity."

The coffee left a taste in the back of my mouth like licking a freshly paved road. I set my cup aside. "I'll go by the motel tonight, talk to Pete."

Woody shook his head. "Give him a day or so to stew. Let him think about shit. He's got decisions to make, and he might want some head space to make them in." He finished his coffee. "You going to the meeting tonight?"

Woody never missed an AA meeting. He had about a decade of sobriety, and he said it was because he was strict to the program. Sometimes it felt as if he lived his life like it was one endless meeting after another. When I'd asked him about it, he said it wasn't far from the truth, but he didn't care, either, since he was sober, and that was all that mattered to him.

"Yeah," I said. "I'm going."

Woody smiled. "Look forward to seeing you there."

CHAPTER 16

I had physical therapy the next morning. I'd started back a few months earlier, as I'd worked to get through the self-loathing that kept me away, and the result was me gradually behaving more like a member of the human race. My limp was faded to an acceptable level. My body ached less than it had in a long time. I could get up and down off of the toilet without effort, which I counted as a win.

Izzy was asleep in the living room when I got home. I thought of the people who came home to pets eager and excited to see them. I came home to Rip Van Winkle with a drool issue.

I cracked eggs into a skillet to fry and dropped bread into the toaster. Izzy, the only creature I'd known who could be awakened by smell, trundled into the kitchen, eyes at half mast, ready for another breakfast. I added an extra egg into the mix; not like she worried about her cholesterol.

After the eggs were all done, I set my food on a plate and dropped Izzy's in her bowl. She wiped hers out in one slurp, and then eyed me, wanting more.

The doorbell rang as I put my plate on the table. I muttered choice obscenities and answered the door.

The guy on my porch was late 40s, broad going fat, in a dark blue suit and a striped tie, with thin graying hair he tried to make the most of. The woman next to him was younger, Black, her hair short and close to the skull, no make-up, dressed in a black skirt suit and a white blouse. She had 50s-style sunglasses on, and he wore mirrored aviators. They were shoulder to shoulder as I opened the door. Only things missing were zippered jumpsuits and signs that read "I'm from the government, and I'm here to help."

"I bet you don't want to ask me about my relationship with Jesus Christ," I said.

The guy smiled; the woman did not. Both took out wallets and flipped them open to reveal badges and IDs from the Federal Bureau of Investigation.

"I'm Agent Burwell, and this is Agent Davies," the guy said. "Mind if we come in?"

"Mind me asking what this is about?"

Burwell took off his sunglasses. "You were at the farmhouse of Tennis McCoy yesterday. Is that correct?"

"I was. I was baking a pie and needed to borrow a cup of sugar."

Burwell looked like a Baptist preacher making house calls. "We're not interested in anything about you, if you're worried about such things, Mr. Malone. But you're a former police officer, so you get how this works."

"That's a lot about me already with absolutely nothing about you."

"That's what the government does. So, about that question of us coming inside—"

I led them into the kitchen. Izzy stood with her front paws on the table, licking the last scraps of my plate clean.

"Goddammit," I said, grabbing the plate. She looked confused, and a little insulted. She sniffed around the top of the table, cleaning off the few bits of egg from the linoleum. I tapped her on the head and she put all four on the floor.

I pointed to the door. "Go," I said, and to my surprise, she did, vanishing around the corner and into the living room to return to her much-deserved sleep.

"She's a big one, isn't she?" Burwell said.

"I ended up with more dog than I've got common sense," I said. "If I ratio-ed those things right, I'd get one of those Chihuahuas you can put in a teacup. Interest you in coffee? The pot's fresh."

Burwell sat down at the table. "I'd appreciate it, thanks. Black."

Davies kept standing, sunglasses still on, every inch of her the coolest customer in the room. "No coffee for me, thanks."

"Well, feel free to take your sunglasses off, since I'm sure the sun isn't much of an issue in here." I poured a cup for Burwell and took a seat. "So where are you guys out of? Clarksburg?"

Burwell nodded and drank coffee. "You were a state cop?"

"I was until I wasn't."

"I read about what happened. It was all in the report on you."

"It's a proud moment in every man's life when he gets his first FBI report."

Burwell laughed. Behind him, Davies stood, shoulder propped against the wood paneling, arms crossed, expressionless.

"What were you doing out at the McCoy farm?" Davies said. Her tone was, if not "bad cop," then definitely "authoritarian cop," which might be redundant.

"I suppose I can't stand by the 'cup of sugar' story," I said. I explained to them about Pete and Isaac. I didn't mention the money. "Tennis said he didn't know where Isaac was, so we left."

Davies said, "That's it?"

"That is it," I said.

"He let you guys walk out?"

"He didn't invite us in for fried chicken, no, Agent Davies, which I had been hoping for. Would have been nice, because I was hungry, and it's obvious my dog eats me out of house and home. So you'll have to forgive me, but I am not sure why the Feebs—"

Davies' eyebrows rose from behind her sunglasses. "Excuse me?"

"Feebs. It's the nickname we always gave you kids when I

was in the state police. You always had nicer cars than us. And better sunglasses."

Burwell sipped his coffee. "Excuse Agent Davies; she's still learning the lingo and getting used to how to deal with people." He threw a look at her over his shoulder I couldn't see, but I could tell wasn't good. Her face tightened and her shoulders shifted and she pulled her arms in closer to herself. When he faced me again, Burwell gave me a half-smile bordering on a smirk, an expression that said, "These bitches, they be crazy."

"You still haven't said why you care about me visiting Tennis McCoy," I said. "I mean, outside of the fact that McCoy's a pot farmer."

Burwell said, "Oh, is Tennis McCoy a drug dealer? I had—"

"Yeah, yeah, you didn't know that, but you can tell me who I banged underneath the bleacher in eleventh grade." I glanced at Davies. "Her name was Angela Callow." To Burwell, I said, "So why are you here? Besides the coffee and my excellent company."

"It's all part of an ongoing investigation we can't discuss," Burwell said. He glanced at my left hand. "Read about that in the report, too."

I held my hand up to my face, peeking through the slit where my ring finger should have been. "None of my gloves fit anymore."

"You got a reputation as a cowboy after that. This a habit of yours?"

I shook my head. "The way I figure, I've only got nine more chances, so why blow them?"

Burwell did most of the talking that followed, asking me general issue questions, stuff about Pete, Isaac McCoy, Tennis McCoy. I didn't like how it felt, but I plowed through, and after a half-hour and a pot of coffee, they were both back on my front porch. Davies hadn't said another word since getting her hands slapped, and hadn't taken her sunglasses off, either.

I stood on the porch with them, looking at the white Ford Focus sitting behind my Aztek. "The motor pool never lets you haven anything flashier for you guys to drive?"

Burwell slipped back on his aviators. "Unlikely. Still better than your ride, though." He shook my hand. "Appreciate your cooperation. You have a great day."

I said to Davies, "Was nice meeting you."

She nodded. "You have a good day, Mr. Malone." She didn't offer to shake my hand.

They drove off, off to whatever exciting adventure was next. Maybe they'd go chase aliens, or terrorists. Or they'd go back to Clarksburg and file paperwork in triplicate. My fingers were crossed on the aliens.

I gave Woody a call after the Feds left and told them what had happened.

"I'd say this confirms the Feds were following Isaac," Woody said. "And it sounds like they're more interested in the marijuana business than in the cryptocurrency."

"I love how casual you say that. 'Cryptocurrency.' Like you fucking understand what it means."

"I understand enough. I've got a Reddit account. People like to talk about those sorts of things."

"Why don't we discuss how come the Feebs came and saw me, and not you?"

"I make a concerted effort to stay out of federal radar."

"There a reason for that?"

"Many reasons."

"Any we can discuss?"

"Nope."

"All right then; we'll put a pin in that for another day. Moving onto Pete and whether we tell him about this?"

"We do. He's got to figure out what he wants his next decision to be about all of this."

"It's a lot to keep dumping on the poor guy."

"He's an adult; we can't make his choices for him. We'll go

out after the meeting tonight. See you there."

And he hung up.

CHAPTER 17

I didn't listen much during the meeting. Me not listening wasn't uncommon; some nights, some meetings, I zoned out. The words would mean nothing, and I stopped paying attention. The meeting was the same people, the same problems, the same issues, the same blame game played out night after night, and everything turned into white noise, humming and buzzing you got used to, almost a dull aching that became somehow familiar and comforting.

But it gave me somewhere to be, and people more clueless than me to be around, and that was often all I needed to make it through the night.

Woody and I brushed off invites from some regulars to go to the Riverside for coffee and pie, and instead we got into the Aztek to drive over to the Days Inn. As soon as we were inside, Woody's hand reached for the radio.

"Don't you dare," I said. I had a Fleetwood Mac CD in, and the thundering drums of "Tusk" had just started.

Woody looked at me like I'd slapped him for stealing cookies. "What?"

"You'll put it on NPR, and I'm not in the mood to listen to people talk. I just spent an hour doing that."

"They switch over to music at night."

"Is it music I'd recognize?"

"You listen to classical music much?"

"I do not. I do, however, listen to Fleetwood Mac, and so we're listening to Fleetwood Mac. When we're in your truck, we listen to NPR, and it fucking drives me insane, but it's your truck, so you can run the radio. This, however, is my car, and I'd like to hear music I can sing along with."

"No one can sing along to 'Tusk.'"

"I'll hum."

I put on my seat belt and pulled out of St. Anthony's parking lot.

We were a block down the road when Woody said, "What are you so grumpy about?"

I tapped my fingers on the steering wheel, roughly in time to the song. "Am I being grumpy?"

"'Grumpy' at the mildest, 'bitchy' at the most honest. You ready to start your period or something?"

We stopped at a light.

"There're times where I come to realize I don't know shit about you, and I'm mostly good with it, because you've saved my life a few times, both literally and metaphorically," I said. "You're smarter than me, you're better armed than most European militaries, you can shoot wings off a fly from a quarter-mile, and you've never talked about anything in your life before you came back to Parker County. I'm okay with all of your mysterious past, since we're supposed to be dealing with the here and the now. But what you did was, you did my thinking for me when Pete offered us money and you turned it down and spoke for both of us, and it pissed me off."

He pointed ahead. "The light turned green."

About the same time, a car behind me honked its horn. I shifted my foot from the brake to the gas and moved us forward.

"I wasn't trying to talk for you," Woody said. "I couldn't take the money, though, because we never did what Pete asked us to do."

"I understand that, but see, you have an actual income from somewhere. God knows where, because again, I don't know what the hell you did before you ended up on a farm where you won't grow anything, living with a million dogs. But me, I'm busting my hump at Witcher Shoals #4 while also being bored off my ass, hoping I can squeeze enough nickels together on a frequent enough of a basis that no one turns off my power and leaves me jerking off in the dark with nothing but my imagination."

Woody ran a hand over his beard. It was grayer than his hair, and as we passed through waves of sodium vapor streetlights, the lines of his face showed more. They were harsh and deep, and they betrayed the possibility of what his years might have been like. They weren't the same age lines I saw in the guys who worked the mines, who packed on 30 years in 10 and looked like grandfathers by the time they had kids learning to drive. These were creases cut into flesh by stress greater than finding coal seams and making weight counts; they were age markers earned in ways I didn't comprehend, and maybe I was better off for it.

"It wouldn't have been the right thing to do simply because it wasn't," Woody said. "Because nothing's only about money. Pete asked for help, and we should have helped him because he needed help. The money, that's secondary. When you do something only because a paycheck is attached, or the promise of a payout, you're riding the line between doing a job and you being a whore. What we could do, and what we can still do, is something good and right in helping Pete. You can say it sounds like fairy tale bullshit to you, but I'm at an age in my life, this is the way I have to be. Just do the right thing because it's the right thing." He looked at me. "If you want the money, you're welcome to it, but that can't be why I do a thing. I've done shit for money, and I didn't like the way it made me feel."

We were at the Days Inn, and I parked. Neither one of us moved to get out, and neither of us looked at the other, and instead we stared forward into the darkness.

"This is an honor thing to you?" I said. "Like you're a goddamn samurai or something?"

"It's more complicated than that," he said. "You'd like the money, but deep down you want to be a cop. You want to feel like what you're doing still matters, and you're willing to replace that missing sensation with money. But my experience is when you replace one thing with another that way, it's all empty. You don't sleep well, and you don't like the face you see in the mirror. You do things because they represent who you are, not because they're replacing who you think you are." He unbuckled his seatbelt. "Let's go talk to Pete."

Pete's car was in the spot in front of his room. I knocked on his door and waited and got nothing. The curtains were drawn, but a light flickered on the edges and I could make out the dulled sound of the TV. I knocked again. Still nothing.

We walked around to the front, to the little restaurant attached to the lobby, checked there but didn't see him. I called his cell phone, and after five rings, it went to voicemail. I gave him another call and got the same response.

Woody brought out a zippered case from his jeans pocket. Inside was an assortment of small steel tools.

"Do you bring a lock pick kit with you everywhere?" I said.

He crouched level to the door lock. "Don't you?"

The motel had switched over to the electronic locks that opened with key cards, but they still had manual locks you could use a traditional key on. Woody fiddled with the lock for about 30 seconds, there was a click, and he opened the door.

The air conditioner was running full steam, and the blast of icy air hit us as we walked in. It was meat locker-level frigid in the room.

The bed was still made, but the sheets were ruffled, like Pete had been laying on top of the covers. On the TV, a bunch of rich-looking women glared at one another. A beer bottle was tipped over on the floor, its contents half-poured into the carpet.

Pete's suitcase sat in the corner, his clothes hanging in the little dressing area. His razor and toothbrush rested on the sink counter. The bathroom door was closed. From within the bathroom, the exhaust fan whined.

"Hey, Pete!" Woody said. "You in the john?"

I walked further into the room. "You ever stayed in a motel and closed the bathroom door when you did your business?"

"Can't think I have."

"Because you don't. Bathrooms in motels are too small, especially if you're a big guy like Pete." I draped a hand towel over the knob and opened the door.

Pete laid in the bathtub, sprawled out, one arm hanging over the tub's edge. His eyes were open, head turned to the door, so it was as if he was staring at me when I walked in. From the middle of his chest, a bloom of blood spread out across him. In the center was a dark, crusty, nearly-black iris, a gaping hole exposing enough of his internal workings to count as an anatomy lesson.

Woody came up behind me and peered over my shoulder. "We should go," he said.

"We have to call the cops."

"And we'll tell them we broke into his motel room and found him dead in the bathtub?"

"But it's the truth."

"How much truth you think matters when someone sees a big old dead ex-cop lying in a bathtub, Henry?"

"What about doing the right thing? All the stuff about honor?"

"Trust me when I tell you there's no honor in people thinking you killed a retired cop."

I heard a knock at the room door. The Parker County sheriff's deputy in the doorway was young and skinny, and the uniform didn't fit him right, like he'd borrowed clothes from his older brother so he could play dress-up. I knew most of the sheriff's department on account of the stuff with the National

Brotherhood, but him I didn't recognize him. He looked new, and a little nervous.

His hand rested on his service weapon in its holster, and his eyes moved from Woody to me to the bathroom.

"Evening, deputy," I said. "What can we do for you?"

"Front desk got complaints about noise, sounded like a fight. Asked if we'd check into it. Mind if I come in?"

"No, not at all."

Woody shot me a look that said I was the stupidest creature to have ever walked the face of the earth, and an embarrassment to the evolutionary process. My expression tried to convey a sense of "what the fuck else are we supposed to say?"

I stepped away from the bathroom door. "We were getting ready to leave, actually."

"This is your room?" the deputy said.

"No, deputy, it is not," I said. "A friend of ours is staying here."

The deputy walked up next to Woody. "I didn't get your name."

"I didn't offer it," Woody said.

The deputy pointed toward the table and chairs near the window. "You mind taking a seat over there for a moment?"

"Are you holding us under suspicion of a crime?" Woody said.

"I'm asking you to sit down for two minutes. I can arrest you, if that's what you want."

"What charge?"

"Since this isn't your motel room, trespassing. Now, please, have a seat."

Woody walked over to the chairs and sat down. The deputy faced me. "Why don't you join him?"

I crossed the room and dropped myself into the other chair. Woody glared at me.

The deputy walked to the bathroom and nudged the door open with his foot and looked inside. Even from across the room I could see his eyes pop open big enough to make Bugs Bunny proud.

Woody set his hands flat on the table. "You might as well do the same."

The deputy pulled his service weapon and aimed it at us. "Hands where I can see them," he said.

"Fuck," I said.

CHAPTER 18

The Parker County sheriff was a guy named Matt Simms. Even though I was tangentially responsible for him getting back with his ex-wife, he didn't seem to like me. As we stood outside of the motel room in the flashing lights of a half-dozen different police cars, and he appraised me with a scorn saved for old women who catch boys playing with themselves, I became positive he didn't like me.

"What the hell, Henry?" he said. "What the fucking hell?"

I hadn't seen him in a few months, and he looked as if he'd lost weight. Simms still carried himself like someone who'd been the high school football star, confident in his motions, but his blue jeans and sheriff's department polo shirt sagged where they shouldn't have, the waist of his jeans cinched up where his belt was too tight. He was further into his 40s than me, his dark hair graying, his patchy stubble even grayer. He wore wire-rimmed glasses, and the eyes behind them seemed tired.

Guys from the county coroner's office wheeled Pete's body out on a stretcher and loaded into the back of a van. One guy guiding the stretcher asked the other about the chances for the Buccaneers to make the football playoffs in the fall.

Woody and I smoked and stood next to Simms' police vehicle, an unmarked Ford Expedition with the lights on the dashboard. Simms leaned on the fender.

"Pete needed help," I said. "He was an ex-state guy from

Morgantown, trying to find a guy who disappeared. He asked me for help, and I got Woody involved."

"You ever thought of staying out of the missing-person business, Henry?" Simms said. "It brings trouble along with it whenever you do." He bought out a notebook from his back pocket and poised his pen at the ready. "Who's the missing guy?"

"Isaac McCoy."

Simms' pen paused in mid-stroke. "McCoy? Of the marijuana McCoys?"

I nodded.

Simms replaced the notebook in his back pocket, shut his eyes and rubbed at the bridge of his nose. "I'm not even going to bother. This won't belong to me in 20 minutes, anyway."

A West Virginia State Police cruiser pulled up at the end of the motel parking lot and Jackie Hall got out. Jackie was a lieutenant with the state criminal investigation unit, and we knew one another from our younger days with the state police. He was a big man, not in a "former athlete" way, but in a "I'd have two of the combos and make them both a 'supersize'" way. The front end of the cruiser rose as he got out of the car. He wore a powder blue short-sleeved dress shirt and a red tie knotted too short to reach over his expanse of stomach, his blonde hair cropped short and plastered flat across his head. He moved like a hippo at its first ballet lesson, arms swinging so loose at his sides they barely seemed connected to the rest of him.

"The motherfucking hits keep on coming," Simms said.

"What's the issue with you and him?" I said.

"We have a mutual understanding where we both think the other one is an asshole. Only thing is, I'm right."

The last bit of words, Simms rushed out, in a hurry to put them in the air before Jackie could hear them. The message was clear: Hate Jackie all you want, but he was state police, and Simms was county. In law enforcement, there was a hierarchy in place, and everyone understood it, especially those hanging from the bottom rungs.

Jackie stepped into our circle. He smiled at me, nodded toward Woody, threw his chin toward Simms.

"Sheriff, I understand you got a dead body," Jackie said.

"Your grasp of the obvious is astounding, Lieutenant," Simms said. "A gentleman by the name of Pete Calhoun."

Jackie's features drew in on one another, as if his nose had become the vortex for a sinkhole. "Why's that name sound familiar?"

"Because he was in the Morgantown outpost same time we were," I said.

Jackie snapped his fingers and the little lights of recognition lit up on his face. "Okay, I remember him now. Paper pusher. Body still on scene?"

"County examiner just took him," Simms said.

"What was he doing in Parker County?" Jackie said.

"He had a private investigator's license," I said. "Came down on a missing-persons."

"What they told me was that he was stabbed, right?"

"You could phrase it that way," Simms said. "You could also say he got carved up, too."

"Found a murder weapon?"

"Nothing yet."

Jackie's gaze shifted to Woody and me. "And what about these two jokers? What are they here for?"

"Because my deputy found them in the room with the body."

Jackie's shoulders slumped forward, as if the structural foundation holding him up had collapsed. "For the love of fuck, Henry, what the hell did you do?"

I took a long drag from my cigarette and blew out the smoke and explained the situation, including the visit to the McCoy farm and the money.

"Your boys find this money?" Jackie said to Simms.

Simms stiffened. "No, Lieutenant, my men didn't find anything, but we will let you know if they do."

Jackie loosened his tie and unbuttoned the top button on his shirt. "This falls within county jurisdiction and everything, Sheriff, but since this is a former state trooper, I'm sure you won't mind if we take the lead on this. No offense, but when you and these characters worked together before, you left everyone else with their dicks in their hands."

"You kids have at this," Simms said. "I only came by because I saw the pretty lights." He fished his keys out of his jeans pocket. "You mind getting your asses off my car? I'm gonna go home and throw rope at the wife."

Woody and I moved, and Simms got in and drove off without another word. Jackie was already on his cell phone.

"Where's this put us, you suppose?" I said to Woody.

"On someone's shit list."

"That feels familiar."

"I'm struggling to remember a time we weren't on someone's."

"It's been a while."

Woody lit a fresh cigarette. "I will concede that going into Pete's room wasn't the best idea."

Jackie ended his phone call and looked at me. "The state superintendent's not thrilled with me, but I owe that to the fact he doesn't like it when former troopers gets killed, queer or not."

"You've taken the sensitivity training to heart, Jackie," I said.

"Henry, I don't care if someone's gay, but it's not my thing, either. I never once looked at a guy and thought 'Yeah, I want my dick in him.'"

"Jackie, when did you see your dick last time? I'm shocked police sketches of it aren't on milk cartons and posters in the post office."

"You've got an abundance of lip for a guy found at a murder scene with a dead ex-cop. You and your buddy over here should be in jail right now."

"I'd be terrible in jail," I said. "I'm a bad man, but I'm so damn pretty."

Jackie's cell phone rang. "You and Mr. Mysterious are free to go, but you're familiar with the routine," he said. "Make sure you're somewhere I can find you without having to work too hard."

"No problem. Wouldn't want you to have to work."

He didn't hear me; he was already on the phone. We didn't hang around to make sure he heard me a second time.

CHAPTER 19

I called up Jackie the next morning and asked him to meet me for lunch at the Riverside. He told me he was too busy to deal with my shit, what with a homicide investigation going on, so why don't I fuck off for a while and try him again when his world wasn't a whirlwind of shit. I said I'd buy, and he told me he'd meet me at noon.

Jackie already had a seat at a table when I walked in, drinking a Mountain Dew and reviewing the menu like it was instructions on disarming a bomb. He'd gotten a table near the center of the restaurant. I took the chair across from him. He wore the same tie as the night prior, but a different shirt, this one blue with pencil-thin white pinstripes.

"The menu at this joint hasn't changed in 40 years, except for the prices, and don't tell me you don't have it memorized already," I said.

Jackie didn't move his eyes from the menu. "I skipped breakfast this morning, so I'm hungry. Buying lunch on your dime means I need to maximize the damage."

"Damn, and I was waiting for the home equity loan to get approved."

The waitress came, and I ordered a Coke and the Reuben and fries. Jackie got fried chicken, an extra side of mashed potatoes with gravy, and collard greens.

"Doesn't the wife have you on a diet," I said.

"She does, when she's looking. She's not looking now."

"How's she doing baby-wise?"

"Good. Seven months. Did I tell you it's a boy?"

"You did not."

"It's a boy."

"Congrats. It's nice when there's an heir to the throne."

"The only throne I'm worried about is the upstairs toilet that keeps clogging."

"Might help if you considered a salad every once in a while."

"Might help if the kid we've got already would stop flushing Legos. Best part is when he gets pissed off after when they're gone. I would bet your left nut that my septic is swimming with those little plastic fuckers. The only good side is it leaves fewer for me to step on barefoot in the dark."

The waitress brought us our sodas and a basket of rolls. Jackie split one in half and spread a slab of butter inside. "You going to ask me about Pete?" he said.

"I was hoping you could suggest lifestyle or fashion tips. Tell me what's big on the runways of Paris or Milan."

Jackie ate one of the rolls. I looked at the three rolls left in the basket, snagged one for myself and set it aside on a napkin. Jackie paused chewing long enough to look at it. "You think I'll take the damned thing?"

"I'm debating on if I want it now or later."

"They're warm now." He finished the roll and grabbed another one.

"What can you tell me about it?" I said.

"About the rolls?"

"About Pete."

Jackie drank some Mountain Dew. "I've had 12 hours, Henry. How much do you think I can tell you?"

"Did you find the 100 grand from Tennis McCoy?"

Jackie shook his head. "Nothing. Even Pete's wallet was cleared out. We're hoping for fingerprints, but those motel rooms are disaster areas for forensics. There could be a hundred different prints in there."

I took my silverware knife and balanced it on one end under one finger, twirling it around with another finger. "What did the Feds say when they talked to you?"

Jackie had a chunk of roll midway to his mouth when he froze. "What Feds?"

"I had two Feebs come by my place yesterday," I said. "A guy and a lady."

The waitress brought our food out. Jackie sat with his plate in front of him, not making a move. This was the longest I'd ever seen a meal stay unmolested in his presence.

"Don't tell me you're not hungry," I said.

He let the roll drop to his plate. It landed in the middle of his mashed potatoes, floating in a pool of chicken gravy. "Why'd the Feds want to talk to you?"

"About Tennis McCoy. They didn't tell me shit, though. Said it was all part of an ongoing investigation."

"Goddammit," he said, almost under his breath. "Goddammit."

"Is this where I intuit that you haven't talked to the FBI? It isn't like I told them anything you didn't know."

"Not the point. I'm just wondering why they came to you before they talked to us."

I shrugged. "The Feds play the game the way they want to play it."

Jackie took a bite of fried chicken. "I don't like it when the Feds come sniffing around. It always means something bigger is going on, and they're not telling anyone, so when things break, we all end up looking like jack-holes and they're the conquering heroes."

I ate a French fry. "Before you feel like the Feds are assaulting your manhood, can we talk Pete?"

"We can, but fuck, Henry, like I said, there's not much there. Everything points neon arrows toward a robbery. That money McCoy gave Pete, it's a motive, but all I have there is your word there even was any money. I'm not holding my breath about trying to ask Tennis McCoy to back up your story."

"None of it makes sense, though. No one knew about the money, no one knew Pete was in town, no one had any reason to think he had money on him. Did you find any sign of forced entry? Any of the guests in the surrounding rooms hear anything?"

"We've got nothing besides you and your sidekick picking the lock on the door and breaking into the room yourself. I'd hoped the motel might have some security system in the parking lot, so we'd get footage of a suspicious vehicle, but the manager said the goddamn thing's been broke for months and the owner won't pony up to fix it." He set down a desiccated chicken leg and shoveled up a forkful of potatoes and gravy. "People in the department, they're rumbling around, saying we should bring you and what's-his-face in for questioning, that you killed him because of a gay thing."

"What the hell does that mean, a 'gay thing'?"

"A lover's quarrel, or he came onto you, and you said no, and you and your friend came back last night and you killed him."

"You're shitting me."

"Nope," Jackie said. "Pete had friends high up the ranks, but no one had a clue he liked taking it up the ass. Doesn't matter, though, because he was a state trooper, and you know how we take this kind of shit. Today, you and Woody are all we've got. We can ID your prints, we have you at the scene of the crime, and a goddamn deputy caught you in the room."

Except for a stack of chicken bones, Jackie's plate was as clean as if it had come from the dishwasher. I looked at my own. My sandwich was gone, and the fries were already cold.

Our waitress refilled our sodas. Jackie ordered a slice of apple pie, warmed, with ice cream on top.

Jackie drank more soda. "I don't believe for a second you kill him, but people don't like dead ex-cops, so they're looking for the easiest answer sometimes. Give me a day or two, and it'll go away. Just don't do anything that makes things even more complicated."

"Me? Would I do that?"

"You could complicate a game of 'Go Fish,' Henry."

Jackie's pie arrived. It was a generous slice, with thin waves of steam rising around a melting scoop of vanilla ice cream.

Jackie's attitude got better, and he smacked his lips in satisfaction at the sight.

"Goddamn," he said, "but isn't that pretty as a picture?"

CHAPTER 20

Woody took a swing at me. I didn't move fast enough to dodge it whole, so the edge of his boxing glove clipped me on the chin. The hit was enough to catch me off guard, and the next punch landed square in my solar plexus. The wind left me, and my knees got weak, and Woody connected a left to the side of my skull. Gloves and headgear on, it didn't matter, because I felt that shit, and it sent me backwards.

I rose my hands in the air. "Gimme a minute."

"Sure thing, Betsy. Gather yourself together."

We were behind Woody's house, sparring. Woody had convinced me I needed to handle myself better if things came down to a fistfight.

"The problem with you guys, used to be cops, is you depend on attitude too much," he said. "You're big, and you're wearing a uniform, so for 98 percent of the public, size and whatever authority you get out of a badge, it's enough."

"The gun doesn't hurt."

"It doesn't, but you don't like them, and you're a shitty shot, anyway. It's the two percent who don't give a fuck you have to worry about, because they're the ones who figure they have nothing to lose, so they'll pick a fight, pull their own gun, take a chance they'll win this one. And the way you are living your life, you keep running into the two percent."

"It must be my winning personality."

Woody was right that almost no one wants to brawl with a state trooper. But it had been a long-ass time since I'd had to worry about that shit, and the price paid for it was I was sluggish and useless in a physical confrontation. Which was why I was letting Woody beat the hell out of me.

That might be an exaggeration. I could tell Woody was holding back. There hadn't been a punch yet that would have thrown my feet out from underneath me. What had connected was more the realization I'd gotten soft and lazy. I tried to comfort myself with the knowledge that at least I wasn't Jackie. It didn't help.

We kept it up for another 15 or 20 minutes, and Woody stayed on me, peppering me with body blows I worked to defend, keeping my forearms tight together and my face protected. I took the hits and sometimes gave one back, and I was grateful when he said we'd call it a day.

As I was pulling off the gear, I said, "Why are we boxing, anyway? It's not like I'll end up in a polite fight. Why don't we do something like Krav Maga?"

"For the same reason you don't take the training wheels off for a four-year-old and expect him to drive a Harley. And where the hell did you hear what Krav Maga is, anyway?"

"One of Ted's girlfriends took classes for it on 'How I Met Your Mother.'"

"You had to Google it, didn't you?"

I pretended like I couldn't, but I heard him laughing. He wasn't shy about it.

I had stopped at Sheetz on the way over and picked up donut holes. We were eating them and drinking coffee in Woody's kitchen. Woody reached into the bag, grabbed one, and ate it whole, licking the glaze off of his fingers.

"Damn, but those are delicious," he said.

"The man who decided we should eat donuts with coffee should have gotten a Nobel Prize."

"Fifth face on Mount Rushmore, bare minimum." Woody ate another donut hole. "I reached out to a buddy of mine, and the Feds who visited you, they check out. They're agents out of the Clarksburg office, with Criminal Justice Information Services."

"That's all fingerprints and criminal histories. Aren't they a data warehouse?"

"Nothing in government only does what they say they do. Back in my day, there were units that claimed they weren't anything more than cooks, and they did a hell of a lot more than ladle out chicken and noodles at Dee-Fak."

"Real world's different from whatever world it was you lived in."

"Less interesting, too. The balance with that is, in this world, you're less likely to get shot or come across dead bodies. Unless one hangs out with your ridiculous ass."

I ate another donut hole. "Let the record show I wasn't the one who wanted involved in this. I was willing to walk away."

"That was never an option. Pete asked for your help. You work with a guy, and he's willing to come and ask for help, you should help him."

"And now we're obligated to figure out who killed him."

"Sam Spade said if your partner gets killed, you need to do something about it, that it looks bad for the detective business."

"The Maltese Falcon, right? I'm sure I watched it with Billy at some point."

"This is where I feel I must remind you the book came first. It's short. Short sentences. You might like it."

I flipped him off and drank more coffee. "Do you think you can live your life based on an abstract moral code pieced together from detective novels and movies?"

"My options are my abstract moral code or the Bible, and I can't get past where you're not supposed to plant two different crops in the same field."

He went to a cabinet and got a legal pad and a pencil. Across the top he wrote "Reasons Someone Would Kill Pete" and drew a line underneath the words.

"Look who's all organized," I said.

"Success in organization is organizing to succeed. We need to get shit straight and work the information we have. What do we have so far?"

"Someone didn't want Pete finding Isaac."

Woody scrawled something on the legal pad. "Which would mean someone followed him to Serenity."

"What if it's Isaac's family?"

"Why wouldn't the McCoys want Pete to find Isaac?"

"They dropped a wad of cash on him like it was gas money."

"Doesn't make sense to kill him. You think Tennis gave Pete the cash, then regretted it, so he opted to take it back?"

Woody wrote that down on the legal pad.

"There's also the matter of this cryptocurrency thing Isaac's involved in," I said.

Woody sipped his coffee. "Back in the day, when I knew a few people who might have wanted ways to move money around without the government knowing—"

"Why do I suspect you knew more than 'a few people'?"

"A handful. Anyway, I'll say something like that would make Isaac quite sought-after by these people."

"To the point they'd snatch him off the street?"

"Enough they'd follow him around for a while."

"So now you don't think the Feds were the ones following Isaac back in Morgantown?"

"I'm saying multiple possibilities exist here. The Feds could want Isaac because of his old man, or because of the cryptocurrency. Conversely, Tennis may have rivals who figure Isaac's the McCoy on the outside, and therefore the easiest one to squeeze, so they could grab him and use him against Tennis. Or they could want the inside line on Cashbyte themselves, and Isaac is the man with the plan in that scenario."

"Isaac seems to have a lot of balls in the air."

“That sounds like a gay joke.”

“Only a little. But this goes back to why I wanted nothing to do with this shit-storm, but there’s this goddamn moral code of yours.”

Woody set the pen on top of the legal pad. “I prefer to think of it as an ethos. Say what you want, but it’s something.”

“What about the Feds? Something’s going on, or they wouldn’t be asking around. And them asking me questions doesn’t mean they want to know what I know so much as they want to figure out if I know anything at all.”

Woody shook his head. “What a tangled web we weave—”

I leaned back in my chair. “Where’s this put us standing now, since now there’s a list of ideas?”

“About the same place we stood at before we had a list.”

“Anywhere on that list did we write ‘Find Isaac’?”

“We should start a second list, with ‘To Do’ across the top.”

“We may want to make that list and add to it ‘Find Pete’s killer.’”

“I’m hoping those are one and the same. I suspect whoever killed Pete doesn’t want Isaac found, and this was a way of discouraging it.”

“One hell of a way of getting the job done.”

“Nothing succeeds like excess sometimes.”

CHAPTER 21

What Woody and I didn't have on any list was a long line of suspects, which meant we needed to go back and cover ground we'd already covered. We didn't have shit to work with, and our best bet was dealing with the McCoys. You don't realize how terrible your choices are when your best option would rather put you in a shallow grave than help. The one thing Woody and I agreed on was that neither of us considered getting shot to be a fun afternoon, so we waited until nightfall to drive out to the McCoy farm.

It made sense at the time.

"You think they'll be more hospitable this time around?" I said as I bounced around inside Woody's truck.

"Our best bet might be they had a big spaghetti dinner and they're all tired."

"Are we hedging our survival on if they're carb-bloated or not? This sounds like a terrible idea, and we should go home before we get killed or arrested."

"Which one of those is your worst outcome for this?"

"They're all shitty ways to spend a night. Particularly the one where we get killed."

"You have no fucking sense of fun and adventure, Henry."

"I've got plenty of sense of fun; I'm almost done with that one zombie game on Xbox."

Headlights cut through the darkness coming up from the

gravel road as we came up to the mouth of McCoy Holler. The headlights belonged to a Ford Focus, and as the car braked to a stop, I recognized the faces of my two new favorite federal agents, Burwell and Davies, inside. The car pulled out and went in the opposite direction of us.

Woody slowed the pickup down as the Focus drove by us.

"Interesting," he said, flipping a U-turn. He idled 30 seconds, then drove off.

"What do you suppose they were doing, visiting the McCoys so late?" I said.

"Maybe the McCoys made too much spaghetti and invited them over."

"What the hell is it with you and spaghetti tonight?"

"I suppose I'm just craving spaghetti. If I had to guess, though, my thought is the visit's about Isaac."

"You suppose the McCoys told them anything?"

"The McCoys aren't known for their kind and loving attitude towards the government. They're the sort who would set themselves up as a sovereign nation if they knew what the term meant."

We kept a reasonable distance back from the Feds' Focus and followed them back into Serenity. They drove through town and into the parking lots for the Serenity Motor Lodge. Woody kept on driving past the entrance. As we cruised by, a head popped up from the back seat. A beat later, the figure in the back seat shoved an ugly-ass cowboy hat on his head.

"Did you see Tennis McCoy in that car?"

"No one else would wear that fucking hat." Woody smiled. "It all grows curiouser and curiouser."

"The term you're looking for is 'more and more fucked up."

"Lewis Carroll didn't have as dirty of a mouth so much as a filthy mind."

"I wish to hell I knew what you were talking about most of the time."

"You should consider reading a goddamn book sometime."

We drove around the block and parked at the bottom of the Wendy's parking lot across the street from the motel. Woody got into the locked box in the truck bed and brought out two sets of night vision binocular. He handed me a pair as he got back into the truck cab.

"You check the first floor, I'll scan the second," he said.

Which we did, sitting there without exchanging a word, watching people come in and out of their rooms and me straining to push back on my bladder, which decided about 30 minutes in that I needed to pee and it didn't care about anything else. I watched the world move through the weird green haze of the binoculars, keeping any thoughts of liquids from my mind.

The silence gnawed at me after a few minutes, but it never phased Woody. He was content to sit without talking, staked out and watching the hotel. He sat there like the snakes you see in pet shops, coiled and seemingly at sleep. Anyone who's ever been in the woods knows among the worst mistakes you'll ever make is to poke at an animal you think is asleep.

After close to an hour, a motel room door opened and Burwell stepped out of the room. Burwell gave the perimeter a scan as someone I didn't recognize stepped out of the room. This guy filled space with a wide chest and broad shoulders and dressed in jeans and an untucked polo shirt that didn't do much to conceal the pistol he had in a belt holster. He stepped to one side of the door, hands folded in front of him. Burwell put his head back into the room, and a moment later he walked out, Davies close behind him, and Tennis McCoy behind her.

Tennis McCoy paused outside the motel room door, looking back inside. Isaac McCoy stepped into the doorway, and Tennis hugged him for a second. Burwell said something and pointed back into the room, and Isaac retreated inside, closing the door behind him.

Burwell and Davies led Tennis McCoy back to the Ford Focus and drove off back toward the McCoys' holler. Then we sat there for a few moments. The muscled-up agent stood at the door, pulled up a plastic lawn chair, sat down, and played on his cell phone.

"Can't say I saw that one coming," Woody said.

"It's like the Spanish Inquisition."

Woody nodded. "No one expects that shit."

CHAPTER 22

The security company phoned me at five in the goddamn morning and told me they were short-staffed and asked me to come in. Despite hating the job with the white-hot passion of a thousand suns, I said I would since it gave me an excuse to get out of my house and go worry about something else besides the various things that didn't make much sense.

I was in the guard shack by 7. The air was already warm and sticky, and I fanned my face with a copy of the Parker County Sentinel-Tribune. They kept Pete's murder on the front page; it wasn't two days old, and there wasn't anything else going on in Parker County. The article rehashed what everyone knew, with a terse quote from Simms about how the Parker County sheriff's department was assisting the state police in the investigation, and a line from Jackie about how the investigation was ongoing. There was no mention of federal agents Burwell or Davies, or of Isaac McCoy.

Mitchell, the asshole with questionable photos on his phone, left the box as I got there, and he gave me a snarled lip and a shrugged shoulder. I ignored him. I'm sure he had other audiences interested in morally iffy celebrity porn.

The day unfurled without hurry. The sun seemed reluctant to launch itself high enough into the sky to burn off the humidity hanging off the mountains, and once it did, it pulsed down in an intensity that bordered on abusive. The sound of four-wheelers in the hillsides cut through the roar of heavy diesel machinery slicing coal seams.

I thought of my own summers when I was a kid, hiking through the hills, getting lost, scratched up on thorns, my clothes ripped and covered in briars. By then, Mom had gone, and it put only Billy and me, and it was obvious he had never intended to raise a child by himself, so he left me to my own devices more than he should have. I'd turned out okay, I suppose, outside of some attitude issues. And a drinking problem. And a divorce. And a lingering sense of loneliness. And no clue what to do with my life.

Maybe I wasn't so okay.

I couldn't have been happier to leave with work if Farrah Fawcett had stepped out of that poster from the 70s and waited for me at my car in all her big-haired, pointy-nippled glory.

I was neither shocked nor disappointed when I didn't see Farrah Fawcett in the parking lot. Instead, I got Matt Simms, planted on the hood of his county cruiser with his feet on the front bumper, drinking coffee from a Sheetz to-go cup. He picked up another cup resting beside him and reached it out toward me.

"No idea how you take yours, so it's black," he said.

"Black's fine."

"Like you like your women?"

"I like them willing; I'm not picky about the rest."

"Perhaps you should be."

"There's a wise adage about beggars and choosers that comes to mind." I sipped my coffee. It was barely below boiling and singed the weakest of my taste buds. "How's your little lady?"

"Rachel's good. She's saying I should get into another line of work."

I popped the lid off the cup and blew at the steam rising from the surface.

"What's she suggest? Selling vacuums door to door? Delivering newspapers? Preaching the gospel of the Lord? You'd look about right behind the pulpit on Sunday morning."

Simms rubbed a hand across the back of his neck, then ran it across the leg of his pants, leaving a damp streak behind. "I'd see myself more as the tent revivalist. Barring those possibilities, I may start up a bluegrass band. Can you steer me in the direction of a good banjo player?"

"Are you required to have a banjo in a bluegrass band?"

"Ever seen a bluegrass group without a banjo?"

"Can't say I've spent much time on the bluegrass circuit."

Simms smiled. "I had a job delivering newspapers when I was about 12. One of the other guys was an old dude, in his 50s, which isn't 'old' anymore based on our now, but when you're 12, that might as well as been 100. The old guy wasn't right upstairs; I don't know if he was born this way, or he took a baseball to the head, or he got kicked by a mule, but he was like a child sometimes. He always insisted the big money was in bluegrass music, how this was the key to getting rich. And this is 1982, so we're all sitting around listening to Billy Idol or Foreigner, and at no point did I ever flip on the radio and the DJ went from Styx to Earl Scruggs. There were never stories about banjo pickers and fiddlers selling out Shea Stadium and women throwing their panties on stage."

"I'll bet that if you're a woman at a bluegrass concert, you're throwing a big ol' set of granny bloomers on stage."

"It's almost a nightmare to imagine. Besides, Rachel's mindset is more in the line of me going into a private security kind of thing."

I tapped the sewed-on patch on my polo shirt. "From personal experience, let me say it manages to both suck and blow at the same time. That's a negatory there, Ghost Rider."

"Her thoughts are geared towards us moving to Charleston when my term expires and working with her brother. He's got this consultancy thing down there, says he's got the work and he needs the extra hands."

"You feeling good enough about where things are, you want to work with the family? You two been back together, what, four or five months?"

"Things are better than before the divorce. I don't live at the office, the way I used to. We both like one another again, so there's a start. She's either gotten better at faking orgasms or I've gotten better at getting her to the station on time."

"Thank you for the worst euphemism for sex I've ever heard."

"I'm spit-balling, Henry. It's been an interminable day. It's been an even longer fucking life."

I drank more coffee. "Someday we'll get to why you came to see me. I'm sure it's not just to bring me coffee, as much as I appreciate it."

Simms pushed himself off of the car. "You want to sit in the AC? I know it's shitty for the environment, but I've got so much sweat running down the crack of my ass, my balls are going to be cooking in soup soon."

"There's a million ways you could say 'let's sit in the car with the air conditioning on' besides that, but I can't imagine one encapsulating it quite the same way. So sure, let's sit."

CHAPTER 23

The AC in the cruiser blasted so strong, the sweat almost crystalized on my face. I half-expected to see sides of beef hanging in the backseat, it worked so good. It was goddamn heaven back there.

Simms had the radio tuned to a country station. I didn't recognize the song, but it sounded like every other song I'd heard on country radio for the past decade. The guy sang about this girl he loved, and how they liked to drive around in his truck, and then a guitar solo threatened to turn everything into a mid-80s rock song, and it got undercut by a steel guitar, and the guy sang more about his truck before going back to talking about the girl. If I'd have been the girl, I'd have been jealous of the truck. I bet he wore tennis shoes with his cowboy hat.

Quieter than the music was the CB radio, which hummed with white-noise static. It was set to the police band, and would burst to life with something from the state police dispatcher before settling back into silence.

We sat with the AC blowing and the music playing and didn't say anything, until Simms said, "I had Feds come by asking questions about you."

"IRS? ATF? Another random set of initials?"

"Can you not do the funny-glib thing and be serious for a few minutes?"

Simms' face was drawn and tired. The skin under his eyes

was loose and the color of plums. He looked like he needed a week-long nap to rest up so he could sleep a month afterwards.

"You don't look good," I said.

"Lot on my mind."

"'Heavy is the head upon which rests the crown.'"

"Did you quote Shakespeare?"

"Your guess is as good as mine. Woody said it once. It seemed to fit," I drank coffee. "You talk to Carl Thompson?"

"About twice a week. He's in Pittsburgh now, in rehab. They say he's got a few months before he comes home."

Thompson had been Simms' chief deputy until earlier in the year, when he'd been shot by the National Brotherhood. The bullets had damaged his spine.

"He going to walk again?" I said.

"No idea. He's stubborn as shit. If anyone can, he will." He looked at me. "He still doesn't like you much. For what it's worth, I don't blame you for Carl getting shot. He does, though, and he's the one who gets to hold the grudge."

"I get a lot of blame for people getting shot, even if I'm not the person pulling the trigger."

"Trouble follows you, Henry. Like stink off rotten fish. And I hope your intentions are good, that you're like the rest of us, trying to do the right thing, and you just end up attracting people who aren't as good of intentioned."

"What if I'm not, though? What if I'm just a greedy guy looking out for himself?"

"Then you're an asshole like the rest of us, and you should keep your fingers out of other people's pies."

I turned down the radio. "What about this visit from our friends, the Feds?"

"It's always pleasant when the guys in the Jos. A. Banks suits show up. Until I met you, I never had much cause to deal with the federal government except to pay my taxes and not vote for president." He shook his head. "You dropped into my world, and it feels as though shit rains from the sky."

"What d'you tell them?"

"That you're a dick, you're a smart ass, I'm not confident you're not crazy, your friend Woody is likely a psychopath, and if I had to, I'd trust you with my life, and I hoped to hell to not have to."

"I appreciate the part about trusting me. Fuck you about the rest. Except about Woody, because he is nuts. The Feds say why they want to know about me?"

"Federal spooks aren't about to tell me anything. They came in, asked their questions, and left. They volunteered nothing. Is this about your dead friend at the motel?"

"Yes."

"Which also has to do with the McCoys."

"Also yes."

Simms stared out the windshield, resting the flats of his hands against the steering wheel. He took deep breaths, eyes closed, sucking air in through his nose and out of his mouth, as he pressed his palms against the wheel. He did this for a minute, opening his eyes again and saying, "I don't need this, Henry."

"I don't think this is anything you've got to worry about, Matt."

"I hope not, because I've got my own shit, without your shit coming into play in my life. Whatever happens with this, I'm not involved. Keep me out."

"You're out."

Simms took another deep breath. He kept his vision focused forward, eyes straight ahead.

"I've got cancer, Henry," he said. "Liver cancer. Stage three."

Simms arced his neck back and leaned it on the headrest behind him. His nostrils flared as he breathed.

"After everything happened with the National Brotherhood, and Rachel and I got back together, I noticed I was losing weight. Then one day Rachel said I looked yellow, and I laughed it off, but she kept on me until I went to get it checked it out. Blood work came back funny, so they did a biopsy, and fuck me running if they didn't find cancer."

"Is it treatable?" I said.

"The doctors tell me it is, but what the hell do they know? I'm on a list for a transplant. They're also talking about maybe slicing off a chunk." He looked at me. "I'm tired all the fucking time. My shit's white, like chalk. I didn't expect it, first time I saw it. I thought I might die from the heart attack from it. Plus, there's the joy of getting jaundiced and turned Asian-looking. I called myself 'the yellow threat' the other day." He laughed, a small, somewhat bitter sound. "Rachel didn't take that comment well."

"I wouldn't expect she would. How's she handling it?"

"How you'd expect if you found out your husband's most likely going to die. She doesn't deal well with the cable going out; this is beyond her capacity to process. She won't talk about it directly, so she talks around it, about how I'll get better, and how we need to think about what I want to do after the transplant. It's why she's pushing me to find another job. She said she thinks we should have a kid." He shook his head. "Me wanting kids was part of why we divorced the first time. She always said she had no interest in wiping someone's ass or making someone's sandwich. Now she's saying a kid would give me extra reason to live. I told her wanting to live is usually reason enough to live. Besides, I don't know I want her having to plan a funeral and a baby shower at the same time. Something could get mixed up and then the kid's traumatized for life."

"If he's your kid, I'm sure that'll going to be trauma enough."

Simms' lips curling upward into thin spirals, his heavy eyes cast down. "You know what I want to know?"

"No. What?"

"You're a drunk, right?"

"I prefer 'alcoholic in recovery,' but we'll go with your terminology."

"I thought it was you guys who liver got cancer. Drunks,

drug addicts, people with hepatitis. The worst I've ever done is take too many over-the-counter painkillers. You, you damn near drank yourself to death, and look at you? Fit and happy and—" He sucked in some air, and the next set of words caught in his throat as he bit at his bottom lip and clutched to his side. There was a groaning noise. He leaned forward and put his forehead against the steering wheel. I could hear him pulling in lungfuls of air.

The song changed on the radio. It was a woman this time, singing about her grandfather.

Simms sat back upright. Thin streams of tears ran from the corners of his eyes. He sniffed and wiped at his nose with the back of his hand.

"How are you doing?" I said.

"Outside of the dying, I couldn't be better."

"This is the stupidest question of the day, but I'll ask it anyway: is there anything I can do?"

He rubbed at his side, around where I imagined the liver to be; it had been a long time since high school anatomy.

"Only if you've got a liver I can borrow for the next 20 years or so."

"I'm kind of using the one I've got." I looked at my coffee cup. "This isn't where I find out you drugged my coffee and I wake up in a bathtub full of ice, is it?"

"I positive that only works with kidneys. But if you're so inclined as to let me try, there's an empty cooler in the trunk, and I sharpened my pocket knife the other day, and I bet we can find you a towel you can bite down on."

"I appreciate the offer, but I'll pass."

"No one else is taking me up on it, either. This is where you figure out who your friends are." He took a deep breath, followed with an exhalation. "I'm afraid you're going to get stuck in shit you won't be able to charm your way out of this time, Henry. The McCoys are trouble on their own, and it's no better when you've got *federales* in the picture. Whatever it is, watch your step."

"Thanks for the warning."

"Not a problem. Has Jackie Hall told you anything with the homicide investigation?"

"Nope. When I talked to him yesterday, the Feds hadn't gotten to him yet. Surprising they talked to you first."

"They're the federal government; they get to do however they want. Now, if you don't mind, get the hell out of my car; I've got paperwork to do before I go home and fuck my wife."

"Do any of your exit lines not involve you having sex?"

"Warren Zevon, when he was dying of cancer, he said you learn to be grateful for every sandwich. I'm trying it out with orgasms. Try to not get killed, huh?"

"I'll do my best."

I got out of the car, and Simms drove off. I took a sip of coffee. It had gone cold. I dumped it out on the ground, threw the cup into a trash can, and drove home.

CHAPTER 24

Woody and I walked out of St. Anthony's after the meeting that night. He had a cigarette lit before we cleared the door.

"How'd he look?" he said.

"The way he looked at the motel the other night," I said, bumming a cigarette. "I think he looked worse because once I knew, my brain filled in those expectations you have when someone tells you they're dying. As soon as he said it, it was like he was weaker, more fragile."

"Simms isn't one likely to pull back from a fight."

He wasn't, but the words still sounded empty. Simms was a brawler, but he was also a guy who had wanted nothing more than his wife back, and sometimes when we get what we want, we don't always know what to do next. Like the dog chasing a car, with no clue of what happens if we catch it.

Woody said, "You hungry? Want to get food?"

I wasn't in a mood to go home and listen to Izzy snore, or to be by myself, either. The meeting had been more useful than usual if only because it offered a vague reassurance about life. No matter what, we were all drunks, hapless about what it took to make the world work, fumbling through and hoping for the best.

Woody mentioned a beer joint outside of town, not too far from Witcher Shoals Mines #4, off the same road to my house. Miners rolled in there after shifts to get burgers. I'd tried them one day for lunch, and the cheeseburgers were great, because beer joint cheeseburgers almost always were. The cook in back pounded out the patties by hand and cooked them on a grill that violated health codes and common sense. The buns were buttered and toasted and there was enough mayo to clog your arteries on the spot, along with a slice or two of melted cheese. It was a thing that made America great.

Woody and I had been there before, even though it was a beer joint. I didn't have drinking memories from there, though, and neither did Woody, so we didn't feel too bad about going. We went for the burgers, and on nights when it looked like the Riverside might be too crowded following the St. Anthony meeting.

I said I'd follow him over there. I trailed behind Woody's Chevy in my Aztek. I needed to find a new ride, since the transmission was slipping. I poured transmission fluid in on the regular and kept my fingers crossed and hoped for the best, which still sucked hind-tit most of the time.

I had all of that on my mind, combined with Bob Seger singing "Hollywood Nights" on the radio, and I guess that's why I wasn't paying attention when the car T-boned Woody.

We were on Rt. 82, about two miles outside of town, when the headlights came on from nowhere, shining like a predator's eyes in the dark, on an exit road off of the main drag. There wasn't much in the way of prelude, just lights and tires spinning and then the car surging forward and slamming into the front passenger side of Woody's truck.

I jammed my brakes in time to watch the car push Woody into the other lane of traffic. That time of night, the road was empty and quiet, and I suddenly became aware of the solitude and the sense of being alone.

The car was an Oldsmobile, 80s edition, an all-steel Toronado with 300-some square inches of engine. The engine roared and the tires squealed as the car pushed Woody's truck into a ditch. I pulled the Aztek over and pulled a snub-nosed revolver from the glove compartment.

Men came out of the Toronado. Two of them walked toward Woody's truck, and one of them came in my direction while the driver stayed in the car. Bulky guys wearing ski masks. I doubted they planned to check if we were okay, or to let us use their Triple-A.

The chunk of road was dark except for moonlight. I aimed at the shadow moving toward me and pulled the trigger. He didn't seem to notice or care he was being shot at. My reputation as a marksman must have preceded me. My hand trembled like an epileptic fit as I fired the weapon and shot after shot whizzed by him.

At less than 10 feet away, I him center-chest, and he stood there for a moment, as if shocked it had happened, before he dropped to his knees and fell over, face first.

I ran toward Woody's truck. Muzzle flashes lit up the truck cab, and then I heard grunting and blows being struck. I picked up a head of steam, moving faster, when the guy I'd shot reached out his arm and tripped me. The revolver flew from my hand, and I hit the pavement. When my bad knee pounded against the blacktop, the first waves of pain and nausea pulsed through me, and it took a moment for me to get my focus back.

The guy I'd shot stood over top of me, grabbed my shoulder, rolled me over, and punched me in the face. He drove an elbow into my gut, and stomach acid surged, and it took everything I had to not vomit. My body involuntarily clenched up, and he punched me again.

"Where is Isaac McCoy?" the man said. He said it with a thick accent. Asian. I wasn't sure if it was Japanese, Chinese, Filipino, or what. It wasn't an accent you got from being in West Virginia.

"What?" I said.

The answer pissed him off, so he clocked me another one in the face. I felt my jaw shift and my teeth grind against one another, and the skin around my left eye tore open. Warm blood oozed out of the cut and down into my ear.

He used the front of my shirt to lift me up off the ground and dropped me back, my head bouncing against the pavement. "Isaac McCoy! Where is he?"

I shook my head, which hurt like hell. "I don't know!"

He slapped me. It hurt less than the punching, if only by percentage points.

"You lie!" he said. "Where is he?"

The other guys stayed busy working Woody over. Someone asked him the same question about Isaac McCoy. Woody asked him if he used chopsticks to jerk off with.

I made a mental note for the next time he gave me shit about saying the wrong thing at the wrong time. Presuming we had a "next time."

My guy slapped me again, to make sure he kept my attention, I suppose. He looked over toward where his comrades were smacking Woody around.

"You and your friend, we kill. You want to die? Homo Isaac McCoy, you die for him?"

"I've never met Isaac McCoy."

"You look for him, though. You and this asshole and the dead homo."

The man hocked up a loogie and spit, missing my face by about an inch, though I still caught a misting across my cheek. "You tell where McCoy is."

I could have told them about Isaac McCoy being in the motel in Serenity, though no way in hell was he still there. They might have stopped beating Woody and me. I guessed if they did, it would be just long enough to kill us. No idea. No matter what, helping these jokers wouldn't be good for Isaac's continued well-being.

The guy growled and pushed himself to his feet. The bullets had blown open his shirt, and I could see his body armor underneath.

The other guys dragged Woody by his ankles from out of the ditch and onto the pavement, about twenty feet away. His eyes were swollen shut, and he smiled at me with teeth covered in blood.

The guy who had worked me over fired off a machine gun-fire of noises I thought were words. The other two said stuff in return.

I coughed up blood and spit it out.

"Hey, Woody!" I said.

Woody groaned.

"How you doing' over there?" I said.

"Never better." His voice sounded thin and weak. "You?"

"Top of the world, ma."

Woody laughed, the laugh turning into a coughing spasm. He groaned again, louder.

"This wouldn't be happening if you'd taught me Krav Maga," I said.

"I'll listen better next time."

Shadows came over me. I saw all three men staring down at me. I smiled. It hurt like a motherfucker.

"Hello, ladies," I said.

Wrong thing to say, I suppose.

All three kicked at me, driving the steel toes of their boots into whatever body part they could connect with. I tried to squirm away, but my body refused to listen to my brain, and the movements I could make hurt too much. They continued kicking me and laughing. A barrage of boots began in my guts, moving up to my ribs, to my face. A rib cracked. I sucked in air and screamed from the pain. And then I stopped seeing or hearing anything, and I became grateful for the reprieve.

CHAPTER 25

Jackie Hall said, "We're looking for the same model vehicles in the area, but I wouldn't put out much hope we'll find anything out. We're guessing they stole it and abandoned it once they finished beating your ass."

I was dressing in the hospital room where I'd been for the past three days. I moved at a pace that would have shamed an arthritic turtle in a body cast. Everything hurt, and if it didn't hurt, it didn't work anymore. A nurse had informed me I had three cracked ribs, and I should consider myself lucky I hadn't punctured a lung. It was all piled on top of the concussion and general issue smacking around, handed out by a handful of angry probable Asians. I needed to find a new definition for "lucky," and a punk band named "Angry Probable Asians."

I looked like I'd lost in the fifth round of a fight with a Mack truck. My face was purple and puffy, and I resembled a pile of bandages and bruises that couldn't blink. They had knocked out a tooth from the back of my mouth, and the doctors seemed to think I swallowed it, so I had that to look forward to in a few days.

"And another thing," Jackie said. He sat in a visitor chair, eating the second Big Mac he had pulled from a McDonald's bag. He had been generous enough to offer me one, but the thought of it made my stomach churn like the *Edmund Fitzgerald*, so I declined.

"Yes, Columbo?" I said.

"About the Asians."

"The Asians? Like, every Asian person?"

"No, only the ones you're saying beat you and Woody up."

"What about them?"

"Are you sure they were Asian?"

"I suppose in the most technical of senses, no. It was dark, and they were wearing ski masks, so all I could see were their eyes."

"Uh huh. And what shape were their eyes?"

"Are you asking me a serious investigative question, Jackie?"

"Approach this from my angle, Henry. Say someone tells you 'Hey, I got the shit kicked out of me by a trio of Asian guys.' You ask them, 'Where at?' They tell you 'On a rural stretch of road in the whitest place on Earth.' Hell, Henry, we don't even have a Chinese restaurant in Parker County, so you're saying Asians are coming here to fuck your shit up when they could make me General Tso's chicken?"

"They sounded Asian, okay? I don't know for sure if they were Chinese or what, but I know they were talking something that wouldn't have qualified as English."

I had pulled out the curtain divider that separated my area from the other bed in the room. The guy in that bed was a fossil already there when they wheeled me in. I didn't know what his problem was since he hadn't said shit in three days and instead kept his TV turned to Fox News and snarled every time someone mentioned Obama. He interspersed it all by regularly ripping out farts that would have discolored paint.

I was putting on my jeans when Jackie said, "Dammit, man, I'm trying to eat over here. No one needs to see your nasty-ass boxers."

"You brought me these clothes. If they're nasty, it's because you got McDonald's on them, and I don't even want to think how some shit like that would have happened."

"Doctors know when Woody will wake up?" Jackie said.

"No idea. They threw out a lot of terms I would have needed a medical dictionary to have understood, but the gist of what I caught involved it being incredible for him to be alive, such as being alive is being hooked up to a bunch of monitors and having a tube shoved down your throat."

What I'd pieced together in the aftermath of it all was that Woody and I had laid there on the side of the road for a while before a car passed by and someone saw us and called 911. It had been a local minister headed home from a church business meeting. The EMT told me later the preacher had stayed with us until they arrived and prayed while they loaded us into the ambulance.

I had to stifle a scream as I pulled a T-shirt on over my head. My arms then didn't want to bend to fit into the sleeves of my other shirt.

"Billy came by," I said as I buttoned the shirt.

"He told me," Jackie said. "He had to let me into your place so I could get your boxers."

"Didn't I give you my house key?"

Jackie shook his head. He finished the Big Mac and wiped up secret sauce out of the box, licking it off of his finger.

"When I came by, you were mumbling shit I couldn't even understand. He said you talking nonsense was normal."

Billy hadn't stayed long. He'd never been a man run over with sentimentality, so he would have wanted to make sure his only child was alive so he'd know if he needed to buy an extra burial plot. Billy would always be a practical son-of-a-bitch that way.

He had picked up my Aztek from the scene and taken it home, however, and had also taken Izzy over to his place. The old man and the dog liked one another enough, I should have been jealous and wondered about my standing in Billy's will.

Jackie fished another Big Mac box out of his bag.

"How many of those goddamn things are you going to eat?" I said.

From the other side of the curtain, a cracked voice said, "Do you mind not blaspheming the Lord's name?" He followed that with a sound like cardboard being torn in two.

The smell drifted our way, and I felt three days' worth of tapioca surge upward, and I worked to keep it down.

Jackie waved his hand in front of his face a few times, then said, "I'm eating this one, and then I'm done."

"Are there more in the bag after this one?"

Jackie couldn't say much with a mouthful of Big Mac.

"I know I'm leaving a bed empty here, but that doesn't mean you have to fill it up by having a coronary," I said.

With a mouth full of half-chewed burger, Jackie said, "Screw you."

There was another crack of thunder from the behind the curtain, and the stench that floated over was like rotten eggs soaked in cat piss.

I finished dressing and said, "Can we get out of here before this old goat gasses us like it's a goddamn war crime."

"Blasphemers!" the old man said, and farted again.

The hospital hallway stunk of bleach and heartbreak, but it was better than the intestinal potpourri in my room. An orderly came by with a wheelchair and told me it was hospital policy he wheel me outside. I told him that wasn't necessary, and he said everyone told him that, but it was still his job.

"Go ahead, old man," Jackie said. "I'll get the car and drive you back home."

As the orderly pushed me down the hall, I peeked through the open doors and at the people inside. It was a creepy and voyeuristic exercise, the vicarious watching of pain. People slept in uncomfortable chairs, necks bent at an angle they'd pay for later. Others gathered around beds, joking and laughing with one another. Some watched TV, or played on their cell phones, while the person in the bed slept.

And then there were the ones wearing their hurt openly, like war paint. Some cried, and others strained to keep it in and failed in the effort. Those were the people who would leave there alone, the last memories of a person tinted by the sounds and smells of a hospital.

We passed by a room and I asked the orderly to stop. I pushed myself up and out of the chair, my muscles and bones screaming bloody murder, and inched my way inside.

The only sound in the room was the steady beep of various devices. Heart monitor. IV drips. The hissing of a ventilator.

Woody was the only patient in the room. His left eye so big it looked as if someone had shoved a golf ball underneath the eyelid. You'd have thought he was dead if it weren't for the slow, rhythmic rise and fall of his chest.

I clinched the bed railing, bit on the inside of my cheek. Felt the rage boiling up inside of me.

"I'm pissed as fuck at you," I said. The words came out harsh, a hair above a whisper. "Because of your stupid ass, I have to go out by myself and do shit I don't want to do. When you wake up, I will beat the fuck out of you."

The orderly was talking to a nurse when I walked back out into the hallway and lowered myself into the wheelchair.

"That's the guy, came in with you after the accident, ain't it?" he said.

"Yeah, it is."

"You guys like—" He paused, wanting to make sure he didn't say the wrong thing. "Partners or something?"

"Friends. He's my friend."

"You hungry?" Jackie said.

"No," I said. "How in the hell can you be?"

"I burn hot. I use a lot of fuel."

"You're a human being, not a goddamn jet airliner. Flights to Tokyo use less fuel."

Jackie was driving me home. Outside the Serenity town limits, into the unincorporated part of Parker County, there wasn't much: mom-and-pop convenience stores, meth labs, and concrete-block bars with beat-up cars sitting in gravel parking lots.

Jackie followed me inside once we made it home. In the kitchen, I pulled a pack of hamburger from of the refrigerator, along with green onions, an egg, and Worcester sauce, and I took the George Foreman grill from a cabinet. While the George Foreman heated, I chopped up the green onion and dumped them into a bowl with the hamburger, some Worcester, the egg, a dash of garlic salt and some bread crumbs and pepper, and smashed everything out into patties.

"You going to cook 'em on that thing?" Jackie said, pointing to the George Foreman.

"That's the idea."

"It drains all the fat out of the burger."

"That's also the idea."

"The fat's the best part. Fat's what actually makes the burger good."

"I appreciate you bringing me home, Jackie, and I'm grateful for you making at least a rudimentary effort to do some police work, but you don't come into a man's kitchen and tell him he's making burgers wrong. Go further south, and you'll get shot for shit like that."

"I'm a hamburger snob. Not like I told you your gravy was too thin."

"Less than an hour ago, I watched you wipe out three Big Macs like they were an indigenous people; you don't get to play the foodie card after that. You'll eat whatever sits still long enough and doesn't bite you back."

I dropped the burgers on the grill and set the tray underneath to catch the fat run-off, and poured us both glasses of sweet tea.

Jackie sipped at his. "So what you going to do now?"

I drank some tea and tried to seem contemplative. "I'm clueless about who killed Pete, and the same with who tried to kill me and Woody. I piece one of those together, I might stumble onto the other. Lacking that, I might go on a rampage of vengeance."

"You want some friendly advice?"

"How much is 'advice' and how much of it is 'this is what you should do'?"

"It's gonna be way more the latter than the former."

"By all means tell me what I should do, then."

Jackie drank more tea. "Stay out of it. Quit. Leave it alone. Walk the fuck away. No, cancel that; run the fuck away, or limp, or hobble, or whatever it is you can manage these days."

"What you're saying, real subtle-like, is I shouldn't get involved."

"That would be the gist, yes."

"And what about this shit? Pete? What happened to Woody and me? Do I go to bed at night and pretend it never happened?"

"Let your wounds heal. Go see a therapist. Get in touch with your inner child. I don't care what the fuck you do so long as you stay out of this and let me do my job. Lest I have to remind you, I'm good at it. Besides that, you shouldn't be fucking with the McCoys, or these rice-eating motherfuckers who already tried to put you in the ground and may try again. There's only one of you walking around now, and you're not even the good one of the two of you."

"What's that supposed to mean?" I said.

"I think it's self-explanatory. Woody, he's all 'mysterious military past.' He's got the guns coming out of every orifice. The ATF would blow a load in their collective shorts at the shit Woody owns that isn't street-legal. Fuck, Henry, he was the one up there in the hill who pulled the trigger on Monica Mayhew, not you. She'd have killed those women that night if not for him. No offense to you, but if I were writing a book about you two, you'd be the sidekick."

Jackie finished his tea and helped himself to more. We didn't talk much after that while the burgers cooked. I had a block of cheddar cheese I needed to use, so I cut thick slices and laid them on the burgers and let them melt, got out the condiments and the buns, and we ate. Jackie said it was a damn good burger. He was right; it was damn good.

CHAPTER 26

The next morning, everything on me ached in ways new and unique to the whole pain experience. I walked so slowly from the bedroom to the kitchen, shadows shifted from the movement of the sun.

The hospital had given me crutches to use, and a cane for when I worked up to that. All I thought of was the months after being shot, and hobbling through life, essentially having to learn to walk again, and the shame that racked me for months, the frustration that had burned at me every time I couldn't move the way I had wanted to.

This wasn't as bad as it had been then—there was no way possible for it to be as bad without lopping my legs off—but I kept having flashbacks to it, and it made me push myself harder than I should.

Izzy stared at me as I worked my way through the doublewide. She must have figured her food bowl would get replenished, and then she got bored and trotted on ahead into the kitchen and laid down on the floor.

"Lassie would have made a pot of coffee for Timmy," I said. "French press."

Her eyes drifted upward toward me, but it was obvious she didn't give a shit for my sarcasm.

I got the coffee started. I suppose I should have stopped there and called it good, but me, being the glutton for punishment I am, decided I also needed to piss. By the time I made it to the bathroom, it had gone from being an urge to becoming a necessity.

I lifted the lid and waited.

And then it happened. From wherever it was inside me that my kidneys are, the burning began. It started as a small ember of warmth, but it spread like a kerosene-fueled wildfire, its fingers stretching throughout my lower body and reaching around and pulling down on my shoulders until my body threatened to double over. I pressed one hand on the wall behind the toilet, pushing to keep myself upright, the twinge of ache in my knees growing until my legs wobbled, and I had to let go of myself and use both hands to keep from falling head-first into the commode.

When the stream started, I wanted to cry. It was like burning knitting needles pushed out of my urethra. My vision blurred, partially from tears, and partially because I struggled to keep my eyes open. Once I got them cranked open, I saw the bright red swirling inside the toilet bowl.

Jesus.

This lasted longer than I thought possible. Cold sweat poured off my forehead, and chills raced through my body, until the final dribble dripped away and my lungs would accept oxygen again. My legs chose that precise moment to collapse underneath me, and I fell backward and forgot there wasn't anything to support me, and I tumbled into the bathtub. I folded like a lawn chair, and my cracked ribs weren't happy about the sudden change, and they offered to puncture an internal organ to get the point across. A scream jumped out of my throat, and I shifted around and pulled my legs in, pushing until my entire body was in the tub.

I laid there for a while. I didn't want to move. I wasn't sure I could. I wondered what would happen if I died there. There were worse ways to go than in your bathtub with your underwear around your ankles, and blood-stained urine in the toilet. Naked and hanging from the hotel room closet was worse. This, though, had to be high on the list.

Izzy came into the bathroom. She stared down at me with those huge brown eyes of her, eyes that betrayed pity, and likely wonder of what would she do if I didn't get out and feed her. She whined and stretched over the edge of the bathtub and licked my face.

I wanted to cry again.

I took my time getting out of the tub and kept the sobbing to a minimum. I flushed the toilet and washed my hands and headed into the kitchen to get my coffee, dreading what would happen when the coffee I was about to drink kicked my kidneys around later.

I drove out to Woody's place. It had been four days, and while I knew Woody had automatic feeders and water bowls set up for his dogs, they still hadn't been outside to do their doggy business, and they'd all be eager for fresh air.

They huddled together, 10 of them, all in the living room, all shapes, all sizes. Pits, German shepherds, beagles, mostly mutts, grouped in a mass of canines on the floor.

The air sat stale and unmoving in the house, and everything reeked of pooch. I didn't smell dog shit or piss—just the heavy, stagnant scent of a lot of dogs. Woody had trained his dogs, and rule one was you didn't shit where you slept. They would have kept it together like there were corks in their asses until they exploded.

Link, the pit bull mix, was curled up in the center. He popped his massive, misshapen head up as I walked into the room and looked at me with suspicious eyes. The rest of the dogs followed suit, giving me long, uneasy looks. The chihuahua close to Link gave me the hardest stare, like he was ready to take my ankles out.

I crouched down, which hurt so much more than it should

have, and whistled, and tried to remember the command Woody had taught the pack. It was something in German. I didn't want to get it wrong, afraid that maybe Woody had trained these guys to rip my balls off if I said the wrong thing.

I said, "Steh! Hier!" Link rose onto all fours and climbed over the rest of the dogs and came over and sniffed me once and dragged his massive tongue up the right side of my face. I must have tasted incredible to a dog.

The others joined, coming over and sniffing me out. Once they realized I wasn't there to rob the joint, they buried their faces into me, eager for attention.

They followed me outside and then pooped and peed everywhere they could. Watching 10 dogs claim their own little spot of land, realizing you never want to walk in that area again, and grass is never, ever going to grow there again, it's something you don't forget, regardless of how hard you try.

The auto-feeder was almost empty, so I filled it, and added water to the other one. The dogs quivered with anticipation at the food. I gave them the command to eat, and they charged like Romans into war.

I sat down in the living room, exhausted. Link wandered in and put his head under my hand. I scratched the top of his skull. He was an enormous dog, and my hand wouldn't fit over his skull. I rubbed his head. It was like petting a pineapple.

As much as I knew I'd never admit it to his face, Jackie had been right. Woody's realm was the "let's go kick ass" thing. I found the trouble, but Woody knew how to fight our way out of it. If I had to handle this, and had to be the tough guy, the best hoped for was not shooting off a toe.

But Woody was my friend. Pete had been a friend. And I needed to do something.

I looked down at Link. "What do you think I should do?"

Link gurgled a sound I interpreted as him enjoying the head rub.

More dogs came into the room and surrounded me. The

chihuahua hopped up onto my lap, did a few spins, and curled up into a circle and fell asleep.

"It would seem," I said, "that this is what I'll do." I let my body relax. "For now."

The dogs got one more round of yard decimation in before I herded them back and locked up. I'd come back tomorrow, and every day until Woody got home. It was the least I could do if I didn't get my rampage of vengeance.

It was almost dark by the time I got back home. I walked up to Billy's house and let myself in.

Billy and Izzy were in the living room. Billy was kicked back in the recliner, snoring. Izzy was on the couch, doing the same. Neither of them flinched when I walked in.

The TV was on, turned to an old black-and-white war thing, with John Wayne storming a beach and killing the Japanese.

I took the remote from the arm of Billy's recliner and laid out on the love seat, my legs dangling over the arms at my knees, and flipped channels until I found something where Liam Neeson snapped necks every 10 minutes, and set the remote aside.

The next thing I knew, Billy was standing over me, saying, "Christ, but you look like shit on a shingle."

I made a good try to stretch, and my body revolted by sending waves of pain throughout every nerve ending it could find, radiating from my core and dispersing it evenly to ensure everything hurt as much as possible.

I got upright and on my feet. Billy watched me through the lens of his thick-framed glasses. "How you doing?"

"Like someone worked me through a washing machine."

"Don't blame you. None of it did much for your looks, either."

"We need to discuss how you can be a supportive and nurturing parent, Billy."

"I took care of the zoo animal you claim's a dog." He jerked his thumb toward the couch. "Damn thing doesn't do nothing but sleep, and she knows well enough she's not allowed on the furniture."

"Then why didn't you move her when you woke up?"

He hesitated for a moment. "I didn't want to throw my back out. Besides, damage is done already. Figure she'll move when she wakes up. She will wake up, won't she?"

Izzy had rolled around a little, but she was still as unconscious as if you'd shot her with a tranquilizer gun.

"Someday," I said.

In the kitchen, Billy poured glasses of tea and we sat at the table. He drank his tea and looked at me and shook his head.

"All joking aside, you look like hell," he said.

"I look better than I feel."

"You must feel awful, then."

"You can't stop using the hammer to drive home a point."

He asked me about Woody, and as I talked, Izzy came into the kitchen. She went to Billy for a moment, then saw me, and rested her head on my thigh. I petted her, and the way she looked up at me, it made me smile.

"She and I should head home," I said.

"Yeah, you should," Billy said. "Looking at you is starting to bother me."

Billy walked me out to the front porch. I asked him if he'd watch Izzy in the morning. He asked me why.

"You going to keep on with this, ain't you?" he said.

"Folks put me in the hospital. I want to ask if their insurance will pay for it."

Billy shook his head. "So what happened, it wasn't enough, was it? You've got a point to prove now? Push it even further?"

"If keeping her is a problem, I'll—"

Billy shook her head. "Drop the beast by before you go. You do what you have to do."

Izzy and I crossed the yard toward my house. We were about halfway there when Billy said, "Henry!"

I stopped and looked back. “Yeah?”

“You be careful.”

“I will.”

“Good. Because I’m not taking care of that dog if something happens. Damn thing would eat me out of house and home.” Billy went back inside, the screen door slamming in the frame.

Thanks, Billy.

CHAPTER 27

I took a self-imposed exile from Morgantown after Maggie and I separated. It was a not-proud combination of self-preservation and cowardice, wanting to avoid memories of the two of us, or that slimmest of possibility of seeing her somewhere. In a college town, there are only so many places to go, and so many places to hide.

But she had moved to Philadelphia. Going on vacations with a new boyfriend. Guess that made everything safe now.

Woo hoo. Goddammit.

Red Salt LLC was in a business park close to I-79, overlooking the Monongahela River. I drove up a narrow dirt road, passing a tall sign with a lot of blank spaces available for company names. A banner at the bottom proclaimed about office space available for lease.

A slick-looking building, long and narrow, gray stone and steel and plenty of windows, rested at the end of a narrow road, encircled by a near-empty parking lot. The lobby was stainless steel and marble, full of vintage-modern furniture not getting much use, all as pristine as a sunrise. The guard at the front desk glanced up from his newspaper long enough to see I wasn't carrying an AK-47, then went back to reading.

I took a two-floor elevator ride up and walked down a hallway as empty and quiet as an Old West street moments before the gunfight. Red Salt LLC was the only name on a door. AC/DC rattled the pressed-wood door, and Angus Young's 30-year-old guitar riffs threatened to throw my hair back once I cracked the door open.

The office's design was by the editors of *Frat House Monthly*. Folding chairs sat in the waiting area. Someone thumb-tacked posters to the wall, all for Japanese horror movies, divided between flicks where a giant creature laid waste to a city, a black-eyed ghost crawled out an air vent, and someone did something indescribable to someone with knitting needles.

I followed the music until I found Patrick Price and Vikram Kaur at desks pushed up against one another, their computers set back to back. The stereo was on a low bookshelf next to the desks.

I knocked on the door. Neither of them moved. I banged on the door harder. They kept staring at their computers. I walked over to the electrical outlet and flipped off the power strip. The computer screens go blank and the stereo went silent.

Price needed to back off the steroids; he was so pumped up, he couldn't drop his arms to his side. If his veins popped much more, they'd be external. He had a neck tattoo now—always classy—of a giant spider web that reached out and across the front of his throat.

Kaur had rounded out, with longer hair aimed in a dozen directions. His T-shirt read "Life Is Simple: Eat, Sleep, Code."

Price raised out of his chair. "What the fuck do you—"

I held up my hand. "Tone it back, 'roid rage. I need to talk about Isaac Martin. Or McCoy. Whatever the fuck he called himself."

Price shifted his shoulders and twisted his head around. The tendons in his neck stretched as he did it, pulsing beneath his flesh like snakes under a bedsheet. The only thing that compensated for the overcompensation was he barely hit five-three.

"Did you find him?" Kaur said. His voice held only a twinge of an accent. "We heard about what happened to Pete—"

I explained the situation. They led me into a converted

makeshift break room. It wasn't anything more than some chairs, a table with magazines thrown across it, and a Keurig. The chairs were green armchairs that looked third-hand from a hotel sale, the magazines about computer technology or wondering when Jennifer Aniston would have a baby, and the Keurig...the less said about that, the better.

Price and Kaur each made themselves cups of coffee. I declined.

Price drank coffee from a Styrofoam cup. "What the fuck happened to your face? You look like you got fucked over with a crowbar and a chainsaw."

"I forgot my spotter at the gym," I said. "Let's talk about Isaac."

Price: We were both taking some boneheaded programming class at WVU. When I'm saying it was "boneheaded," that means I aced through the fucker. I'll own I'm not the brightest guy in the room. Vikram—

Kaur: You can call me "Vikki." Everyone does.

Price: Yeah. Whatever. So, Vikki, he kicks my ass. I'm good, but Vikki, he's better than I'll ever be. He can do shit you wouldn't think possible in code. But then there's Isaac.

Kaur: Isaac's different. Not like, because he's gay, because we never cared about that.

Price: What two guys do, that's their own business. What two girls do, fuck, let me watch! Am I right? Right?

Kaur: Anyway, as good as I am, and understand that I am very good, Isaac's brilliant. Professors told us Isaac's one of the best programmers in the country. He could do so much. The CIA or NASA came calling for him. He could make bank for these giant corporations. You name it, and Isaac could write his own ticket.

Price: And that's why Vikki and I never understood what made Isaac to want to hitch to our wagons, except I think maybe he liked the autonomy. Charting his own course, setting his own sails, that kind of shit.

Me: Did Isaac ever talk about his family? His past?

Kaur: Never. He discussed nothing in his life before he came to WVU. Very much a tabula rasa.

Price: What Vikki said. We were all in Discrete Math together. Me, that wasn't my strongest point, but Vikki's a whiz at that shit, and we hung out, and Isaac was a lost puppy almost, and we dragged him in, and we all got along.

Me: How did Cashbyte start?

Price: Senior project. About the time the Bitcoin started, and everyone was losing their shit, going on and on about how it would change the world. We wouldn't need banks anymore, and it would democratize finance. Which is bullshit because money is money is motherfucking money, and you can't democratize that base of human need, I don't care what you call it. There's always gonna be someone who's got a lot, and there's gotta be a lot who have nothing.

Kaur: Cashbyte started out as somewhat my idea—

Price: If you say so, sure.

Kaur: What's that mean?

Price: It means, sure, if that's how you want to roll with this, go ahead.

Kaur: I don't understand what you're inferring, Patrick.

Price: I'm not inferring shit, Vik. I'm saying flat out Cashbyte wasn't your idea.

Kaur: Then whose was it? Are you going to say it was yours?

Price: Do you not remember us sitting around that night, talking, we got stoned, and I said, "Guys, we need to come up with our own Bitcoin"?

Kaur: That's as if a man who stared up at the sky and thought, "Someday, it would cool to go to the moon," he should get credit for NASA. I wrote the first code for Cashbyte.

Price: You overwrote the first code for Cashbyte, is what you mean to say.

Kaur: Fuck you, Patrick. I didn't see you adding anything of substance to the process—

Me: Ladies, chill the fuck out and figure out who's got the biggest computer dick later. I need you to focus important shit. Tell me about Cashbyte.

Kaur: Anyway, yes, we were like many people, trying to figure out how to capitalize on the desire for the next electronic currency. Are you familiar with how Bitcoin or Cashbyte works?

Me: In the vaguest way possible.

Price: Okay, this is the "big picture" way of looking at it. Bitcoin, Cashbyte, cryptocurrency as a whole, all operate differently from the way money's operated in the past. Cryptocurrency eliminates the need for banks. With almost any form of payment these days—outside of cash—there's a trail that goes back to banks. Bitcoin uses shared public ledgers called block chains, and that's how the transactions are recorded. Those public ledgers are on the computer systems of people who want to get involved in Bitcoin.

Me: Why would someone want to get involved? Just out of the goodness of their hearts?

Price: You ever known anyone to do anything out of the goodness of their hearts if they could get paid for it?

Kaur: The way Bitcoin works, and Cashbyte operates this same way, is the various computer systems process the transactions, their reward is they receive Cashbyte currency. Bitcoin releases new Bitcoins every 10 minutes, and it's distributed to the users based on the amount of work done by the systems through a process called "mining." Makes it sound like something's really happening, like you're an old-time prospector. Cashbyte releases every fifteen minutes.

Price: That was my idea.

Kaur: (eye roll)

Me: But there's no actual cash, coinage, anything like that, for any of these.

Kaur: There are physical representation of Bitcoin because people are old-fashioned, and we like something weighing down our pockets, but those tend to most be use for memorabilia's sake. In its purest form, digital currency should be nothing more than ones and zeroes.

Me: Then what's to keep someone from writing ones and zeroes and creating their own counterfeit currency?

Kaur: That is the beauty of the code, and the shared nature of cryptocurrency. Picture thousands of computers all operating the required software, and they must all share consensus on transactions. Any transaction that tries to break the rules and doesn't meet the needs for the entire system is rejected.

Price: And there's a finite amount of the currency, released over a finite period. When the endpoint for release comes, end of fucking story, there is no more. You can't print new, so it's not affected by inflation in that way.

Me: Then what makes Cashbyte so special that people want involved?

Price: Secrecy, brother. See, everyone likes to talk about Bitcoin like you can do whatever with it, that it's all anonymous, but that's bullshit. There're bits of information attached to every Bitcoin. Maybe not bank information or Social Security numbers, but there's always something, because this is the twenty-first century, and nothing's private anymore. The Feds can subpoena records and, if they want to work hard enough, they can trace back Bitcoin to users.

Kaur: People were using Bitcoin for things like buying drugs or weapons online, through what they call "dark webs." People counted on Bitcoin being anonymous, and they found it wasn't when the police showed up at their door.

Price: What we wanted was to make a cryptocurrency that was truly anonymous. That you could spend with total impunity and never let it trace back to you.

Me: Which makes it sound like you're fine with your financial Frankenstein being used in illegal activity.

Price: Liberty is neither easy nor cheap, man. Cash spends whether you're dropping it down a G-string on Saturday night or in the collection plate on Sunday morning.

Kaur: Our idea was never to spur the currency's use in criminal activity; when we began, it was an interesting project. As I said, I wrote the initial code for Cashbyte—

Price: After I came up with the idea.

Kaur: (sighs) And then Isaac, he came along and...I can't even tell you what he did to it, because he took that groundwork and made the whole project into something beautiful.

Price: Isaac rewrote Cashbyte to be 100 percent anonymous. He created code so transactions were encrypted and then mixed into other users' payments, so it is impossible to follow who made what payment. The system acknowledges payment was made. No electronic trail left behind. End of fucking story. It's better than cash, man. It was code that would almost bring tears to your eyes, it was that hot. Any hotter, I'd have fucked it and given it my real number to call me the next day.

Kaur: Jesus, Pat.

Price: Just saying.

"Aside from its fuckability—" I said.

"That was it," Price said. He was on his third cup of coffee, sitting on the edge of his chair, eyes big and his body alive with caffeine, nervous energy, and other things I didn't want to think about. "This is totally anonymous spending, plus it's more stable than Bitcoin."

"Bitcoin value fluctuates wildly," Kaur said. "Cashbyte mirrors sensible economic patterns and will not rise and fall with the tides."

"Is that why investors want in on it?" I said.

"Yes. Cryptocurrency mining requires a lot of computer processing power, but Cashbyte less so, which means if you get a greater return on investment setting up more powerful servers. This is why Japanese investors want to set up the first round of processors, to be on the Cashbyte ground floor."

"But they won't do it without all three of us, and Isaac, well, fuck, he's the brains here," Patrick said.

Kaur cast a sideways glance at him. Patrick was too jacked up to notice.

"What's happening with the Japanese investors?" I said.

Kaur said, "They are getting antsy. We've been getting phone calls."

"Anything suspicious?"

Price and Kaur traded off looks that screamed "Suspicious? What do you mean by 'suspicious'?"

"I guess they have been getting anxious," Price said.

"They tried to kill Pat," Kaur said.

Price smacked Kaur upside the head. Kaur drew back a fist like he would take a swing.

"The fuck, dude," Kaur said.

Price snarled and started out of his chair. "We agreed to shut up about that."

I snapped my fingers. They froze and looked at me.

"You girls can battle it out later," I said. "Tell me what happened."

Kaur dropped the fist and said, "It was when Isaac didn't show up for the meeting, and we were freaking the fuck out, I won't lie, because these guys—"

"The Japanese," I said.

"Yeah. We'd talked the day before, and he knew we were scheduled to meet with Wakahisa."

"Bailing out on a commitment, Isaac wouldn't just do," Price said. "He's hardcore about meeting deadlines, meeting commitments. Plus, he's got that vibe with the Japanese way more than Vikki or I got. Things got to be a particular way with them. Everything's about respect with them."

"When did the Japanese investors show up bearing cash?" I said.

"February," Price said. "We were looking for venture capital to get the thing going, and Cashbyte was getting attention, but no one was willing yet to throw us a few million dollars to get started."

Kaur said, "We were still coding out of my apartment when there's a knock on my door, and standing there is this Japanese guy, and he's got bodyguards, and he says he's looking for the people who make Cashbyte. He's dressed to the nines, and he carries himself like he's someone with power. He said his name was Wakahisa, and he fronted for a business interest that wanted to pump money into Cashbyte."

"Which you accepted without question."

"Fucking A, we accepted it," Price said. "Dude wrote us a check that day. Got us this office space and the Keurig and everything."

"Money well spent, clearly. This 'business interest,' did you ask about it?"

"Their fucking check cleared; that answered any questions we had," Price said. "Things have been going well since, while we've been working all the bugs out of Cashbyte, but then they pushed for a go date. We told them there were delays."

"Caused by?"

"Glitches we've been trying to solve," Kaur said. "Like with the wallet."

"I thought it was all electronic," I said. "What do you need a wallet for?"

Price said, "A wallet for cryptocurrency stores the information needed for transactions with that currency. It can be software on your computer, an app on your smartphone, or even a key fob. We were having issues with security standards, and Isaac, his head wasn't in the game, you could tell. Wakahisa demanded a meeting, and Isaac was a no-show."

"How'd they respond when Isaac wasn't there?"

"Poorly," Kaur said.

"How poorly?"

"They tried to kill Patrick."

Price hit Kaur again on the head. Kaur punched Price in the

arm. It was like a mosquito body-slamming an elephant.

Price tried to smile away some embarrassment. "We had a misunderstanding, nothing more—"

"They tried to push him out a window," Kaur said.

"Goddammit, Vikki—"

"Wakahisa always has these big guys with him. They look like thugs, and we thought it was because he's rich, they're bodyguards. But when Isaac didn't show, Wakahisa's men got very upset. Wakahisa said Isaac was vital to the project, demanded we tell them where Isaac was."

"I tried stalling them, putting everything off," Price said, "but it was too late in the day, and cancelling, they would see as a show of disrespect. We told them Cashbyte was far enough, we could focus on things without Isaac. They didn't agree."

Kaur said, "Out of nowhere, one of the goons grabs Patrick by the neck and pushes him out the window."

"It's a cultural difference, that's all," Price said. "Business rolls different in different places."

Kaur stared at Price. "Dude, do you see the color of my skin? Do you think I'm unaware of 'cultural differences'? My whole life is 'cultural differences,' and there's no culture where you try to shove someone through a window because you don't like how a business deal is going."

"Did you go to the police?" I said.

"And tell them what?" Price said. "That we're getting threatened by shifty Japanese businessmen over digital currency? You think the rednecks around here give two fucks about that shit, or even understand what we're talking about?"

"When did you talk to Wakahisa last?"

"Two days ago," Kaur said. "He told us we had three days to find Isaac or he'd take Cashbyte from us."

"It's not his to take," I said. "How can he do that?"

"His tone was that we didn't have a choice," Kaur said.

CHAPTER 28

The FBI's CJIS center in Clarksburg sits on about 1,000 acres of land the government bought in the 1990s after Robert C. Byrd, West Virginia's favorite political son and the then-chair of the Senate Appropriations Committee, negotiated a multi-million dollar federal facility hundreds of miles away from Washington. It was a sly move on the old goat's part, and the joke for years was he settled for this when he couldn't get a submarine base.

You pass Clarksburg on the interstate coming down from Morgantown. There was a 7 p.m. AA meeting at an Episcopal church there in town. I'd hit it a few times in the past when I'd been in the area. I took the exit and decided on a whim to go. Sometimes hearing the woes of a different group of drunks is a good thing.

The group met in the church library, a nice change-up from basements and Sunday school rooms. It was an oak-paneled room, the lighting a little softer, the shelves lined with books that asked why God let bad things happen, about how stupendous He was, and the need for a kingdom in the Middle East.

Folks were friendly, and a few people remembered me, or they were at least nice enough to fake it and ask me how I was doing. They saw the bruises and the bandages and asked me if I was okay. I lied and told them I was doing aces and poured myself a cup of coffee.

The library door opened as the meeting started. Agent Davies, dressed in blue jeans and a V-neck T-shirt, headed straight to the coffee, made herself a cup, and sat down. She sipped her coffee and saw me sitting across from her. I threw a nod in her direction. She turned and talked to the woman sitting next to her.

A guy in a gray suit and an expensive haircut led the meeting. His name was Alan, and he had six years of sobriety, and it looked to agree with him.

We went around the circle and talked. I passed on my turn. When it came around to Davies, she rested her forearms on the table and said, "Hi, my name's Taylor, and I'm an alcoholic. I'm glad to be here, because who knows where I'd be if I wasn't here. Steve Martin's got the line in a movie where he says, 'I'd rather be here with you than with the best people on Earth.'" The joke drew laughter from the group. Her face softened as she told it, and she passed on to the next drunk.

They sent the basket around and we all threw in our dollars and rose and joined hands to say the Lord's Prayer. The meeting broke up and everyone headed outside to pollute their lungs. I bummed a cigarette and was taking in the chemicals as Davies came outside. She talked to another woman and walked by me without a second glance. She took long, intent strides toward a Toyota Camry. I pulled a last drag off my cigarette and smashed it underneath my foot and followed her.

"Taylor!" I said. "Taylor!" She didn't slow down, and she didn't turn back. She brought out car keys from her jeans pockets and hit the button on the fob to unlock the doors.

"Agent Davies!"

She froze and turned and faced me with fierce, narrow eyes.

"Mr. Malone," she said.

"It wasn't Steve Martin," I said.

"Excuse me?"

"The joke you told in your share, it wasn't Steve Martin who said it. It was Fred Willard, in the movie."

A faint smile crept out from the corners of her mouth. Her

eyes widened. They were hazel-colored, softer than expected. She didn't wear much makeup. She couldn't have been more than 30, tops.

"Yes, it is," she said. "Tell me this is an incredible coincidence, Mr. Malone."

"A hell of a one."

"You look horrible."

"Thanks. Literally everyone I've talked to for days has been kind enough to tell me I could frighten small children. I'm glad you're as charming in your off-hours as you are on the clock. How long you have in the program?"

"Thirteen months. I'd had three years before, but shit happens, you know."

"I know all about the happening of shit. So, Agent Davies—"

"It's Taylor. I don't bring up work at meetings. A history of drinking problem clashes with government security clearance."

"I imagine it might."

"I hope you won the fight."

I smiled, and the effort hurt. "You should see the other guy."

"Does he look worse than you?"

"No, actually. In fact, he and his friends got clean away, but they almost killed me and my friend."

A flash of something passed over Davies' face, betraying a feeling she had stepped into something.

"I'm sorry," she said. "I should go—"

"Before you leave, Taylor, is there any chance of you telling me what the hell is going on with Tennis McCoy."

The moment of regret vanished, and she snapped back into business mode. "This is an ongoing investigation, Mr. Malone. I can't discuss it."

"I can appreciate that, except I have one friend who was murdered, another who's in the hospital, I'm walking around like the Elephant Man, and there're questions I can't help but feel you might have answers for. Also, if it's all the same to you, everyone calls me Henry."

She shook her head. "I appreciate your circumstances, Henry, but there's nothing I can tell you."

I leaned in toward her. She pivoted her body away from me.

"Then tell me why you had Isaac McCoy in a motel room in Parker County," I said, "and you and Burwell drove Tennis McCoy around like Miss Daisy headed to the store."

She pulled away so fast, you would have thought I'd tried to lick her ear. Her expression bunched everything together until you couldn't quite make her features out, but it didn't mask that she was pissed.

"I don't know what you're talking about, Mr. Malone," she said.

I put on my sweetest smile. "It's Henry, remember. We're friends now."

"I've got to go, Henry."

"I'm sure you do." I watched as she got into the car. The engine came to life and the motor on the power windows whined as the driver's side glass slid down. She had her sunglasses back on, even though most of the sun was already behind the mountains. This was the Agent Davies I had met at my trailer: aloof, unreadable, unknowable. She looked in my direction for a moment, then pulled out of the parking lot and drove away.

CHAPTER 29

Because I had nothing else to do, I dragged myself to work the next morning, though my body protested the entire time. I sat in my little booth, contemplating the swirling vortex of craziness making up my life at the moment, when my cell phone rang and a blocked number appeared on the screen.

Under normal circumstances, I never answer those, because there's never anything good on the other end of a blocked call. I answered it anyway. What the hell, I felt like living dangerously these days.

Before I could say anything, a woman's voice said, "Mr. Malone?"

"Yes?"

"It's Agent Davies."

"How d'you get my cell phone number?"

"I work for the government, Henry; this is what we do. I could also tell you the last 10 porn sites you jerked off to if I wanted to."

"I'd recommend against that."

"I was making a point. Are you working today?"

"I'm at work, though I'm not sure I'd call this 'working,' per se."

"What time do you leave your place of employment, then?"

"Four. Why?"

"Meet me at six." She gave me the name of a 24-hour

laundromat in Bridgeport.

"Hell of a drive from Clarksburg to wash your delicate underthings."

"Can you do this or what?"

"What it 'this'?"

"'This' may have answers you want."

"Then I suppose my next question is 'why are you doing this?'"

"Because sometimes your career is going too well, and you need to fuck it up a little. See you at six."

She hung up.

Laundromats are depressing. There are few things more disheartening than gathering in a communal area with strangers so you can wash and fold your T-shirts.

The faces are almost always the same. There are mothers who seem as if they're dancing on a razor's edge between leaving the snot-nosed kids on the floor as they scream they want a bag of Funyuns and bringing out a tranquilizer gun. There are old men who split their attention between the TVs mounted beneath the ceilings and the endless rainbow of clothes running circles in the dryers, and their expressions say they can't keep up with the plot of either. Over there will be a young couple, rail thin and happy, blissfully in love, playfully throwing her thongs and B-cup bras at one another, without a clue that adulthood and high-waisted full-cut panties are in their future.

The sign in the window of the Bridgeport laundromat advertised free Wi-Fi. Inside smelled of heat and laundry sheets. A group of young Mexicans huddled in a corner, talking in rapid-fire Spanish. An old lady with expertly coiffed white hair sat in a plastic chair, reading a women's magazine that offered 40 Fourth of July recipes guaranteed to make the family celebrate.

Davies was emptying a dryer into a basket when I walked in. She hoisted the basket over to one of the folding tables and motioned me over with a jerk of her chin. She wore a Coca-Cola

T-shirt and black yoga pants.

"You invite me to the most interesting places, Agent Davies," I said.

"The heating element on my dryer is out, and I'm waiting for the part to come in so I can fix it." She folded and stacked her clothing so neatly, the kids at H&M would have been jealous.

"You fixing it yourself?"

"I'm sure as hell am not paying someone 65 bucks an hour to do it. YouTube exists for this reason."

"I'm impressed."

"Don't be impressed when a woman can fix stuff, Henry. It makes you sound like a jackass."

"I'm so glad I drove out here so you can insult me and I can watch you fold your underwear."

"You're a big boy. I'm sure you're familiar with women's underwear."

"I had a solid standing on the matter at one point, but of late it's been an academic study, lacking in the way of field research."

"Sorry to hear that. My fiancé is fond of my underwear."

"Awesome. Thrilled for him. Can we get to the brass tacks of why you asked me to come out here?"

She moved on to blue jeans. They were faded from the factory, with rhinestones and other sparkly shit all over the back pockets.

"Did you follow Agent Burwell and myself the other night?" she said.

"I did. A friend and I."

"Who's your friend?"

"You're the government, remember? You know what I had for breakfast this morning."

"Oatmeal and buttered toast."

"How the hell did you do that?"

"Lucky guess. Actually, we know you associate with someone named Woodrow Arbogast. I also know your friend Arbogast enlisted in the Marines after high school. Beyond that, there's not much about him. His records after enlistment and basic are classified multiple levels beyond my access. I have top secret clearance, Henry, which means your friend operated on things my boss's boss can't access. That's interesting, don't you think? It makes you sort of interesting by proxy."

"I'm fascinating regardless, Agent Davies. Lots of things in life are interesting, though, such as what the hell is going on that the FBI has Isaac McCoy in custody and you and your partner are chauffeuring around his marijuana-growing father to see him?"

"You're a 'cut to the chase' sort of guy, aren't you?"

"I'm an 'I'm tired of getting fucked with' sort of guy."

"Isaac McCoy is under FBI protection as part of an ongoing investigation into the use of digital currency to launder drug money."

Davies had emptied her basket and everything was folded and stacked on the table. She placed everything back into the basket and hoisted the basket into her arms. "Come on," she said. "I'll explain this at my place."

I followed her. After all, she had nice underwear.

CHAPTER 30

Davies lived in a freshly painted blue split-level with flowers blooming in the beds that lined the walkway. She had me pull in beside her yellow VW Beetle in the garage, so my Aztek wouldn't be out on the street.

"Do you think someone would connect we're talking?" I said.

"No," she said. "Your car is ugly as fuck, and I don't want the neighbors complaining it's dragging down property value."

The kitchen was done in yellow—daisies and chickens—and had one of those racks dangling from the ceiling where you hung shiny copper-bottomed pans you never cook with. Davies told me to help myself to the Keurig while she took her clothes upstairs. The coffee selection was overwhelming, with ten or twelve types of pods and names for them like Sumatran Blue and Vanilla Hazelnut Espresso, and all I wanted was something that said "coffee-flavored coffee." In the back of the cabinet I found an unopened box of Eight O'Clock pods. I dropped it in and waited the two minutes and took a drink of the finished product. Somewhere, Juan Valdez and his donkey spun in their graves.

Davies came back down and made herself a cup of something that smelled like cinnamon and almonds. She leaned against the counter, arms folded across her chest. She was toned and sinewy; occasionally the muscles throughout her upper arms involuntarily twitched. Even now, relaxed, she was all business.

"How long have you got?" she said as the Keurig gurgled and hissed behind her.

"About six months. I fell off the wagon in December."

Davies' coffee finished. She added honey and milk to it. "I've read files on you and your friend Arbogast."

"Just call him 'Woody.' Hearing him referred to as 'Arbogast' is weird as hell."

"His file is pages and pages of blackouts. So many secrets your friend must have."

"If you're so interested in Woody, go talk to him—once he wakes up, that is."

"Would he answer my questions?"

"I wouldn't count on it. But you're a good-looking woman, so who knows."

Davies laughed. "Mr. Arbogast would be great if I had unresolved daddy issues, but I'm good there, thanks, and besides he's not my type. And he's only related to this because you're related to this, and it seems you got dragged into this only because of your prior relationship with Pete Calhoun."

"Let's not bring the word 'relationship' into this. All I ever did was work with Pete."

Davies arched an eyebrow. "Did Calhoun being gay bother you?"

"I didn't find out about Pete being gay until a day or so before someone killed him. Even then, I didn't give a shit. Pete loved Isaac. That's all I need to know. Speaking of Isaac, how is he anyway?"

"Mr. McCoy is doing well, considering circumstances. He broke down when we told him about Mr. Calhoun. He was—" She twisted her mouth, like she struggled to make the words fit. "Higher-ups in the Bureau feared he might back out after he was informed of Mr. Calhoun's death, but I didn't feel this was information we could keep from him."

"Awfully kind of you, treating him like a human being. So what's his role in this money laundering thing? I'll presume this is about Cashbyte."

She nodded. "Ears went up at CJIS when word came out about Cashbyte and its security features. We've been on cryptocurrency watch for years now, since the onslaught of dark web sites and use of digital currencies to launder money from criminal activities. A lot of money goes through Mexico these days, sometimes the Middle East, and the cash lost along the way in the laundering process ends up in the hands of terrorist groups and drug lords. Guys like that, they're popping huge boners at the thought of something like Cashbyte."

"What's your interest in this, though?" I said. "I don't follow how cryptocurrency is in your wheelhouse."

"CJIS is what the title says: 'criminal justice information services.' Fingerprints, criminal backgrounds, historical data, you name it. But the Bureau knows cyber-based crime is everywhere, so almost any office has a unit tucked away that focuses regionally on those threats. Cashbyte would have been on FBI radar regardless, but because it was in the CJIS backyard, they assigned us to monitor it. These kids created a cryptocurrency almost handcrafted for money laundering. Someone decided there was one of two ways to handle it: squash it, which would have opened a shit-storm of controversy, or use it to our advantage."

She sipped at her coffee. "Washington told us to go talk to Isaac Martin, nee 'Isaac McCoy,' since it was clear he was the principle behind Cashbyte, and he was the asset who might be more cooperative with our efforts. We approached Mr. Martin, nee McCoy, and asked him to add lines into the code which would allow the government to track transactions, to allow us to monitor illegal activity."

"Which would make Cashbyte a de facto government currency."

"Correct. We wanted an 'Abscam' for the electronic age, to create a ground-floor long con to open the doors to bust organizations we couldn't get a foothold into. But the code couldn't just be good; it had to be perfect. It had to be written in such a way that someone who broke it down line by line wouldn't figure out we had reworked it. No one would trust something like this blindly. The cartels would hire people to strip the code bare and try to find backdoors, find the little extras we wanted Isaac to place in there."

I finished my coffee and set the cup down. Davies asked if I wanted another cup. I said no.

"Tell me how this is legal? The government tracking those sorts of private transactions. Because I wouldn't imagine it would only be the bad guys using Cashbyte."

"We're fighting a war on terror, Henry, and that fight sometimes involves tactics people don't like. Those tin-foil-hat conspiracy websites are more right about things than they imagine. But our focus isn't on private citizens; it's only on suspicious transactions connected to criminal activity. The concern isn't on someone buying pot for their own use; it's on the group trying to transfer millions of dollars in profits from heroin trafficking, or a sleeper cell looking to buy radioactive material to build a dirty bomb."

"And how did you get Isaac to sign up on this?"

"Our approach to Isaac appealed to his patriotism, his sense of right and wrong, his desire to help keep his country safe."

"Did your approach also involve Tennis McCoy?"

"We may have hinted Mr. McCoy's father was under surveillance by the DEA, and his cooperation could help those problem go away."

"You blackmailed him."

"Tennis McCoy is a criminal, Henry. Mr. Martin was more than happy to become part of this process."

"I'm sure he was. Everyone loves it when the government shows up knocking on the front door. But he's not a criminal, so why keep him under federal lock and key?"

"We received intel of a heightened criminal interested in Cashbyte. The probability was a criminal group or groups wanted to make it their own. The risk was too high; Isaac's life was in danger."

"Would have been nice if you could have shared this information with his husband; his internal organs might not have been splattered all across a motel bathroom."

Davies looked into her coffee cup. "Mr. Calhoun's death was unfortunate—"

"'Agent Davies, your milk spoiling is 'unfortunate.' A flat tire is 'unfortunate.' Someone gutted Pete and left him dead in a bathtub, and if you and the rest of your stooges had one ounce of common decency among you, he might still be alive. So with all due offense, you can take your 'unfortunate' and stick it up your ass."

The front door opened, and a woman's voice called out.

"Honey, whose piece of shit is in the garage? Did you finally call the guy to fix the dryer?"

Tiny feet made a mad dash into the kitchen, and a little girl, about four, a head full of blonde curls, wearing a Disney princess T-shirt and blue jean shorts, threw herself around Davies' waist. She clutched a piece of paper that she shoved up toward Davies' face.

"I drew an elephant!" she said.

Davies lifted her up and kissed her on the cheek. The girl wrapped her arms around Davies' neck and looked at me and furrowed her brow, then relaxed and smiled and held her picture out in my direction.

"I drew an elephant," she said again. "Wanna see?"

I took the paper she handed me. There was a gray circle, some black lines that were probably legs, another circle with a curl coming off of it, and everything was five or six colors. It could have been an elephant, with some imagination. And then I realized I was critiquing a kid's drawing, and what kind of a dick did that make me?

"It's beautiful," I said. "I bet it goes on the refrigerator."

"Thanks. Who are you?"

"This is a friend of mine," Davies said. "His name is Henry.

Can you say 'hi' to Henry, Emmy?"

"Hi," she said, and reached her hand out toward me. I shook it.

"Wonderful to meet you, Emmy," I said.

A woman walked into the kitchen. She looked about 40, with razor-straight blonde hair, a slight tan, dressed in jeans and sandals and a tank top that showed off a trim physique and toned arms she used to carry in groceries in reusable cloth bags. She paused in the doorway when she caught sight of me.

"Hi," she said. "Are you here to fix the dryer?"

"Not if you ever want it to work again," I said.

The woman walked up to Davies, and Davies tilted her head behind Emmy and kissed her.

"This is Henry Malone," Davies said. "Henry, this is Felicia Meadows, my fiancée. Henry is part of an investigation I'm working on."

Felicia's expression suggested I wasn't welcome. It further suggested she might bash me upside the head with one of those shiny copper-bottomed pots. She threw a glance over at Davies. Davies talked to Emmy about her picture. Felicia placed the grocery bags on the counter.

"This is one of those things you can't talk about, right?" she said as she emptied a bag, setting everything down with slow, deliberate movements. She all but slammed cans on the marble countertops.

The tension filled the room like carbon monoxide in a garage. I got the hint.

"I should be on my merry way," I said.

Davies put Emmy down. "Go play in your room, and Momma and I will get dinner made."

Emmy dashed out of the room. Davies watched her, then looked at Felicia. Felicia kept her back to us.

Davies said, "I'll walk you out."

***

Davies led me back into the garage. She hit the button at the entrance from the house, and the garage door slid open. A Subaru Outback blocked me in.

"Not a word about two lesbians and an Outback," she said.

"That was nowhere near what was going on in my head," I said. "Plus, that's the worst sitcom title ever."

I was almost in my car when she said, "You want to talk to Isaac?"

I looked across the garage at her. The FBI training, the training that teaches you to be a badass, that had gone, and Davies looked soft and a little sad, like her heart was breaking for a reason I didn't want to know.

"I want to know who killed Pete," I said. "If talking to Isaac does that, then yes. But what you're talking about is a big no-no, I'd imagine."

"It's a massive no-no, but after breaking this many rules, why stop now?" She swiped a set of car keys from a hook next to the door. "I'll call you later to set up a time."

"Thank you." I glanced back toward the door, and inside the house. "I hope everything's good with you and your girl."

She didn't even look at me as she walked toward the Subaru. "It's what it is."

CHAPTER 31

Dinner that night was one of those stir-fry kits where you added chicken into a sauce that was a color that didn't exist in nature. The mess was food in the legal sense, but I stopped being hungry once I had it on my plate, and I pushed everything around until it turned cold and gelatinous. I scraped what remained into Izzy's bowl. She had no complaints, licking the last molecules of sauce off of her face once she was done, and then stared up at me with eyes that asked why there wasn't more.

I debated on what stupid decision to make next, and called Maggie. She picked up on the third ring. I guessed she was home from the sound of the TV in the background.

"Henry?" she said. "Everything all right? Is Billy okay?"

"He's fine. He's old and grumpy, but he keeps waking up every morning."

"That man will be around to throw dirt on your grave."

"The way things look lately, you might be correct."

"Jesus, Henry, what are you getting yourself into now?"

"Nothing, Magpie. Nothing at all."

Everything got quiet. I thought the call had dropped.

"Maggie?" I said. "You still there?"

"Yeah. I'm here. 'Magpie.' Wow. Haven't heard that in a month of Sundays."

"Sorry. I didn't—"

"No, no, it's fine. You're the only person who's ever called me that, is all."

"That's what makes it a pet name, Maggie. If everyone called you that, then it wouldn't mean as much."

"True. It's so goddamn personal. Intimate."

"Which we're not."

"Divorce makes things significantly less intimate."

I walked into the kitchen and started a pot of coffee. I didn't even want the goddamn coffee, but I needed something to do, and I lacked for other options. Woodworking would have been too loud and awkward.

"Can I ask you a question?" I said.

"You're going to, regardless of if I say 'yes' or 'no,' so I'm not even sure why you'd preface it."

"Always the problem with you fucking journalists. So literal minded."

"Ask your question, Henry."

Izzy wandered into the kitchen doorway. She wore a literal hangdog expression like she was embarrassed for me. I neither needed nor wanted my dog's pity.

I said, "This guy you're seeing—"

"Goddammit, Henry."

"Wait. Give me a second. This guy you're seeing. How serious are you?"

The connection got quiet again. I fought the urge to push, to fill in the silence.

"There's something," she said. "Neither one of us are rushing to define the thing, but it's something. Please don't ask me if I love him."

"I'm not sure I'd want the answer to that question."

"What about you? Are you seeing anyone?"

"I tried. Didn't do well. The market is tough in small towns for gimpy, nine-fingered ex-cops."

"I bet there's a dating site for that."

"And porn. About the guy—"

"You don't quit, do you?"

"In all these years, Magpie, ever known me to quit?"

"Not even when you knew better."

"Do you work with this guy?"

"I do. He's an editor at the paper here."

"Is he why you moved?"

"He's not. I moved because I was tired of Morgantown, and West Virginia, and I needed the change. The fact he was here already didn't hurt."

"He drink?"

"He does."

"You still drinking?"

"I am. Does that matter?"

"Probably not, but in my head, it might."

"Your head is a dark place to be, Henry. You drinking wasn't the problem. You not drinking wasn't the problem, either."

"What was the problem then?"

"The problem was us. Or the problem was you and me, because there wasn't an 'us.' You changed after the shooting. I told myself you'd be okay, that you'd pull your shit together and do what you needed to get well, but you didn't. You fought it. You couldn't be a cop anymore, so you made yourself miserable, and you made me miserable. And when you stopped drinking, it got worse, and you blamed me for your unhappiness. The only moods you had left were resentful and angry. I hit my limit, and for me to drink away my hurt would have killed me. But I'm well aware what a bitch this makes me, because I'm the woman who left her wounded ex-cop husband after he got sober. I'm the person you root against in a movie. But our marriage stopped feeling right for me, Henry, that's all. The space your anger took up left no room for me."

A voice in the background said, "Honey, everything good?"

Maggie moved her mouth away from the phone and she said, "Yes, it's okay. Can you give me another minute or two?"

I said, "Jesus, but he's there. I—"

"What would have changed, Henry? Would you have

stopped?"

"Maggie, please."

"Sign the papers, Henry. We sent out fresh copies the other day."

"I'll check the mail for them. Thanks."

There was a pause, and she said, "You planning on staying in Parker County?"

"I don't know," I said. "I could be close to putting together something resembling a life here."

"That sounds good, Henry. I know there's plenty on your plate by being there. Billy can be a trip. Plus the stuff with your mom."

"That's shit to deal with regardless of where I am."

"Are you getting into another situation, Henry?"

"What do you mean?"

"That you think trouble finds you, when the truth is you invite it over. You let those doors fly open and usher it on into the room, ask it how it takes its coffee."

"Things are happening, but I've got it under control."

"Can you do me a small favor?"

"Sign the papers. I will."

"No, you asshole. Don't die."

"I'll see what I can manage."

"You do that. I've got to go."

"Have a good rest of your night, Magpie."

"You too, Baloney."

The line went dead.

Baloney. Talk about pet names. She'd called me that after our second date.

I couldn't help but smile, even as I stared at the cell phone in my hand and tried to not think about what might be happening in Philadelphia.

CHAPTER 32

Davies called me after 11. The news was on, but there wasn't much of anything to tell, so they filled up the time with stuff about the heat and a Little League team collecting cans for charity and Serenity becoming a sister-city with some place in Eastern Europe I'd never heard about.

Pete's murder got a brief mention. No "there's no new information." Mostly "he's still dead," which didn't seem like news. Him not being dead after being dead would have been different.

I answered the phone.

"Agent Davies," I said. "How's the home front?"

"It's been better. Partners are never happy to find mysterious strangers standing in the kitchen."

"I don't guess there's any cold comfort in the fact you're playing for the other softball team, so to speak, so the best I can offer is the hope you'll let me watch."

"If that were any more cold of comfort, I'd need a parka. What are you doing?"

"Watching the news."

"Anything interesting?"

"A church group is selling homemade chocolate banana pops so they can go to Africa and give villages mosquito nets to fight malaria."

"I guess not, then."

A vehicle pulled into my driveway. Izzy, vicious watchdog

she was, snored next to me on the couch.

"Hold on," I said. I opened the end table drawer and took out a .45 and walked to the front door. Headlights approached from the distance. I slipped my finger into the trigger guard. A car stopped in my driveway, the headlights went dark, and a figure stepped out.

"There's someone here," I said.

"I know, dumbass," Davies said. The figure waved at me as it approached the house. The closer it got to the light, the clearer I could see it was Davies.

I walked out on the porch. She looked at the gun in my hand. "Do you think you can please not shoot me? I'd appreciate it."

She wore jeans and a Bluetooth earpiece and a light jacket to cover up her shoulder holster. Her eyes were glossy and rimmed with red. I disconnected the phone call.

"You okay?" I said.

"Great as so long as you don't shoot me."

"I think we've established no one's getting shot tonight."

"Night's still young."

"Hope springs eternal. What's wrong?"

She rubbed at her eyes with the back of her hand. "Nothing. Why?"

"Because while I'm not the sharpest pencil in the drawer, I can tell you've been crying, it's after 11 on a school night, and I'm positive you being here continues to violate Feeb protocol."

"You live to dog-pile the shit on, Henry."

"I'll mention you're the one who pulled up in my driveway and almost got shot."

"You doing anything right now?"

"Besides talking to you?"

"Besides that."

I shook my head. "The guy who isn't Johnny Carson is getting ready to come on."

She shoved her hands into the front pockets of her jeans.

"Price and Kaur are dead," she said. "Someone broke into Price's apartment tonight and shot him, execution-style. Kaur got into his car, turned the key in the ignition, and it turned into a fireball in his driveway." She twisted her head around until her neck cracked. "You want to come and talk to Isaac McCoy?"

"I do."

She motioned toward the trailer. "Then put your gun away, please."

"Yes, ma'am."

"We moved McCoy this morning to a safe house outside of Clarksburg," she said as we hit the interstate. We took her VW.

"It's a safe house within spitting distance of a major FBI facility," I said. "You should re-evaluate the term."

"Proximity can be important. We use it to store assets before depositions and trials."

"'Assets'?"

"Witnesses. Informants. Whatever you want to call them."

"I like the term 'people.'"

"Sometimes, the individuals in question barely qualify as human. Major players. Linchpins in criminal organizations that would make the Mafia blush."

"Is this guy Wakahisa part of one of those types of organizations?"

"I guess Price and Kaur told you about him."

"They did. They said it was implied he would kill them if they didn't move faster on Cashbyte. I'm also confident his guys were the ones who came after Woody and me."

"Wakahisa isn't what we would term a player yet, but he's on the rise upward. Reports have him now as a guy with money and an affection for having bodyguards. He specializes in financing criminal operations and then laundering the resulting money."

"He's not Japanese mafia then? What is it called, Yakuza?"

"You watch too many movies. Wakahisa is strictly out for

the highest bidder. There's not much in the way of Japanese mafia activity in West Virginia, what with the absolute lack of, you know, Japanese people in the state."

"Don't be such a smart ass, Davies."

"Coming from you, that's funny. No, Wakahisa has been moving into digital currency for a few years now. Cashbyte is the perfect option for him. It lets him develop a business model where he can do transactions across the globe without worrying about law enforcement being on his ass."

"He figures if he controls Cashbyte—"

"He can charge for its use. The anonymity could make it the go-to for anyone trying to move money without detection. You're talking about the possibility of tens of millions of dollars a day, and Wakahisa can charge a few pennies from each dollar for the privilege, which criminal organizations will do because it's cheaper than traditional money laundering costs. You lose in the basic individual costs, but your volume goes up exponentially."

I said, "Why are you doing this?"

"Driving? Because I know where we're going."

"You're violating I can't even fathom how many forms of protocol, and I'm not sure why. Based on a surface judgement of you, I'd have guessed your career means more than this."

"I don't like how this has played," she said. "It's felt wrong for a while. Calhoun's death was a tipping point. I read the autopsy report. You were right in what you said at the house, that no one deserved anything like that." She glanced down at the dashboard clock. "We're almost there."

I had more questions, but I didn't ask them. I guessed they were questions Davies wouldn't have wanted to answer.

CHAPTER 33

The street was quiet, since it was after midnight and sane people were asleep, dreaming about the sex they weren't having, or living lives that didn't involve keeping their lips puckered up and pressed against the boss' ass. Me, I was noticing the number of houses on the street with "for sale" signs in the front yard.

"This place didn't take the turn in the economy well," Davies said as we parked. "Kind of like everyone else, people bought more house than they could afford, then figured out there wasn't any way they could pay for it in this lifetime."

We walked across the street to a small two-story house, blue with red trim, the lawn well-kept and green. Hedges were boxed off as if someone had used a level and a ruler to keep it even. In the streetlight's glow I saw flowers in the boxes that ran along the walkway leading up to the front door. Part of me wished I knew what types of flowers they were, but now didn't seem the right time to Google it.

"One of our agents, he enjoys landscaping, so he volunteered to do the lawn upkeep on the place," Davies said. "We won the neighborhood association award last year."

"My mom had a green thumb," I said. "I found a scrapbook once, these newspaper articles about flower shows she'd won around the county, in the state. She was quite the thing in that little circle of people."

Davies pressed the doorbell. She gave two short rings, a long ring, and then two more short bursts. "You get any of that skill?"

"I killed a plastic fichus once."

A litany of locks clicked, there was a faint beeping noise, and the front door opened enough for a sliver of light to escape. A man's voice said, "Hello?"

Davies flipped open her ID and held up to the crack. "Thanks," the man said, and opened the door. He looked fresh out of the academy, with a military-grade buzz cut and even less fuzz on his face. He cast a look at me. "Who's with you?"

"A consultant on the case," Davies said. "He wants to speak with the asset. I'm vouching for him."

"That's against policy, Agent Davies. You're aware of this."

"I do, and thank you for you reminding me, but I will ask you to let us inside regardless."

"I could be in a lot of trouble for this."

"Tell them I overpowered you."

The young man smirked and stepped aside. He wore a Rush T-shirt, cargo shorts, and shoulder holsters with two nine millimeter pistols.

The agent closed the door behind us, twisted the locks and punched in a code on a keypad next to the door frame. "The asset is in the living room, watching TV."

I said to Davies, "The man has a name."

Davies and the man exchanged glances. "Civilians," she said. As if that explained anything.

In the kitchen, two agents stood around an island, eating sandwiches and playing cards. Both wore jeans and polo shirts and shoulder holsters, like they were heading off to play a round at the most hostile golf course in the world.

We walked into a large living room with a giant wall-mounted TV. The guy who wasn't Johnny Carson played beer pong with Jennifer Lawrence. Somewhere in the recesses of my heart, I ached for a barely sober Ed McMahon, Doc Severinsen's ugly suits, and Joan Embry from the San Diego Zoo, with an animal that might kill Johnny, or at least pee on him.

Isaac McCoy stretched out on the couch, staring at the TV without interest, not because he cared who won beer pong but because there wasn't anything else on. If I hadn't known better, I would have thought he was checking out Jennifer Lawrence's boobs. I would have been. Maybe he was checking out the guy who wasn't Johnny Carson.

"How you doing, Isaac?" Davies said. Nothing. Davies cleared her throat. "Isaac?" Still nothing. Louder, she said, "Mr. McCoy?"

"I heard you the first two times, Agent Davies," Isaac said, his focus never veering from the TV.

The young agent said, "He's been like this since—" The words cut off sharply.

Isaac remained motionless on the couch. "Yes, I have been remote since my husband died," he said. The voice may as well have come from a statue. "Imagine that. How bizarre is it that I would have an emotional response to my husband's death, and I can't do anything except sit here with strangers with guns who stand around and refer to me as an 'asset,' like I'm a goddamn gold brick?"

Isaac hurled the remote across the room. The action startled the agents, and their arms reached across their chests, palms open to take hold of their weapons, acting as if by cardiac muscle. The remote shattered against the wall into pieces of plastic and microprocessors. McCoy's void expression crumbled like ancient stone, and his face flushed red, and tears raced down his cheeks.

"And then my two best friends die," he said. "No. They don't die. They were fucking executed. I'm sitting here, and everyone I care about is dying!" He choked the words out in thick-breathed gasps, saliva foaming out of his mouth, and pushed his face into his hands and cried.

I sat on the couch next to him and laid my hand on his back. He turned and buried his face into my shoulder and threw his arms around me and cried even harder. The sobs were loud, each one a tiny, piercing jab into a part of me I wanted to forget about, but instead it stirred awake and hurt in ways I'd forgotten possible.

Davies and the young agent worked to look at anything else but this. Neither of them said anything.

On the TV, a band I didn't recognize was playing a song I hadn't heard before.

I let Isaac cry until he was done. It took a while. The guy who wasn't Johnny Carson went off, and the guy who wasn't David Letterman came on.

Isaac's face was puffy and red and wet when he pulled away from me. He wiped at his cheeks and the corners of his eyes with the back of his hand. On the front of my shirt, where his face had been, there were wet spots from tears and, I'd have bet, snot.

He swallowed hard. "I'm sorry."

There was a box of Kleenex on the coffee table, and I handed it to him. "You're good."

He pulled a bunch of tissues from the box and blew his nose.

"I'm Isaac," he said.

"Henry. It's good to meet you, Isaac."

"You with the government?"

"I'm not. I was friends with Pete."

Isaac's eyes turned bright and he bit on his bottom lip. He balled up the tissues tight into his hands. "How did you know Peter?"

"From his days in the state police. He came to Parker County looking for you, and he called me asking for help."

Isaac got more tissues and wiped at his nose. "I thought I'd get the chance to tell him, when this shit started, I wanted to let him know I was okay, but they said it was a bad idea, for his safety. They showed up and said I had to go."

Davies said, "Security concerns dictate we didn't have the time for the farewells everyone would have liked. It's all imperfect. We do the best we can."

I started to say something about the quality of their "best," but something flashed in the corner of my eye. Davies saw it, too, and her body tightened into battle mood.

A light through the living room window. Movement in the yard.

Davies had her pistol in her hand. The other agent had taken a firing position, aimed toward the door.

Isaac said, "What's happening?"

Davies motioned to me with one hand, keeping her pistol trained toward the window.

"Get up. I need you moving now."

I grabbed Isaac and pulled him to his feet.

"Get him in the kitchen," Davies said. To the young agent, she said, "Give him your other gun."

From the hallway, the young agent focused on the front door. "I can't do that, Agent Davies."

"I'm not asking." Her eyes flashed toward him. "You can still tell them I overpowered you."

The young agent unholstered his other pistol and handed it to me. "You know how to use one of these?"

I flipped off the safety, pulled back the action and racked a round in the chamber. "I've watched a lot of Bruce Willis movies."

"Yeah, just try to not fucking shoot a good guy, okay?"

Davies said, "There's a door in the kitchen, looks like a basement. Leads downstairs into a panic room. Code's four-four-nine-four. Get him—"

A figure dressed in black, with night vision goggles glowing in the darkness, appeared at the window. He stuck something on the glass. There was a flashing red light and a beeping.

Davies pressed her hand against my shoulder, pushing me out of the room. I dragged Isaac out with me as the explosion rattled the house, shook the floor beneath our feet, and the window shattered and blew inwards, turning into a million slivers of glass.

CHAPTER 34

What happened next:

It's all in five seconds. Or five minutes. Somewhere in between.

Front door, another explosion.

Someone screams.

Gunfire. Automatic weapons. The screaming stops.

Davies. "Move! Move! Move!"

Me, pulling Isaac behind me.

The kitchen. Two ways in. Agent at one entrance. Davies at another.

Davies. "Get him downstairs."

The panic room door. Other end of the room.

Outside. Weapons firing. Bullets strike the kitchen windows. Bulletproof glass.

The rattle of gunfire. Far kitchen entrance. The young agent dances. Collapses into a pool of his own blood.

Two men, wearing ski masks, stand in the doorframe. Machine guns and bulletproof vests.

My gun raised into the air. I don't think. I react.

Aim.

Fire.

One shot. Boom. The bullet hits the man square center of the forehead. His head jerks backward, and the rear of his skull explodes, sending blood and chunks of brain across the wall behind him.

Somewhere, surely, angels sing at this miracle. Which is fucked up, but oh well.

The second man drops to his knees as I pivot my aim at him and pull the trigger. My bullet lodges into the doorway. Because you only get that lucky once.

He unleashes a wave of gunfire, tracing a pattern toward me as I fall to the floor. There're more shots fired behind me and the path of the man's machine gun arcs upward and into the ceiling as he screams and a plume of blood pulses out from the side of his neck like a gusher of oil. He drops his weapon and folds his hands over the wound as blood spills all over the tile floor. There's another shot that goes through both hands. He stumbles and slips on his own blood collapses backward. He hits the floor with a thud and his head bounces and cracks. The bone of his skull shattering is audible over the surrounding gunfights.

Davies stands behind us with a thin wisp of smoke trailing up from the barrel of her pistol.

The panic room door. I pull at the knob but it doesn't turn. There's a keypad next to the door, with a small yellow light above the keypad.

Davies. "Type in the goddamn code!"

I punch in the numbers. *Buzz* and the light turns red. I key the numbers again. Another buzz, and the light remains red.

Me. "It's not working."

No emotion from Davies. No time. There's shit to do.

Davies. "You, Isaac, back here."

Isaac is on the floor, like a cat, on all four, ready to pounce. He springs to his feet. Back to Davies. Me, right behind him.

Davies reaches into her pockets, hands me her car keys. "I'm cover fire. You and Isaac run for it. I'll follow."

There's gunfire outside, staccato bursts of machine guns, answered with repeated shots from semiautomatic pistols. Wailing in the distance, police sirens.

Deep breath.

Me. "Let's do this."

Isaac, right on our heels. Race to the door. Bodies fill the hallway. Jumping over them. Blood smeared down the wall. Everything stinks of copper and gunpowder. My knee hurts. Of course it does. Fuck.

At the front door. Sudden silence. A quiet that makes my stomach drop. The sirens getting closer, the blue lights growing brighter in the inky sky.

Deep breaths again. Quick glances at one another.

The yellow VW, across the street. Fifteen yards away. Maybe. Shit. Fifteen yards. Seems like fifteen miles.

Davies pulls a cell phone from her pocket, hits the "push to talk" button. "Floyd? Mathers? You there?"

A man's voice. "Mathers here."

"Where are you?"

"East side of the house, ma'am."

"There's two friendlies down inside, at least four hostiles down inside. What you got as a count?"

"One friendly down, two hostiles."

"Floyd down?"

"Yes, ma'am."

Davies. A grimace. Tight jaw. Exhale. "We're exiting the building. Cover us."

"Yes, ma'am."

Davies steps out the door. Isaac follows right behind her. I pull up the rear.

Every step we take on the porch squeaks a floorboard. There's a dead man staring at us with empty eyes, half of his body sprawled across the swing.

We clear to the porch steps.

Davies. "We'll run for it."

Me. "Woo hoo."

On the walkway. Feet barely touching the cement. Almost to the sidewalk. Fractions of seconds here. For this moment—only this moment—I am grateful my physical therapist is a goddamn masochist, because I am almost running like a real human being.

There's a gunshot. There's a sudden, intense burning in my left arm.

I spin and fire blindly. There's a silhouette standing somewhere in the yard, and then it's not standing anymore. It makes a noise, a grunt, and collapses to the ground. I see the gun in its hand, and there's another shot from it, but it misses by a mile, and goes over our heads. I shoot again, hit again. This time I see the spurt of blood.

Davies. "Mathers!"

She stops and runs toward the silhouette. In the light, now I can make out a face. It's the agent who let us into the house. He's nothing but a fucking kid.

Davies, to the agent. Standing over him. He's lifting the gun at her. She roundhouse kicks him in the side of the head. The gun goes flying. He lands on his side.

There's a silky warm wetness running down my arm now. I touch it and pull back fingers covered in blood. The wound is worse than a grazing, better than an entry wound, and hurts like a motherfucker. In the great symphony of life which is being shot, with having your knees taken out via a shotgun being the "1812 Overture," this is a community orchestra violin solo. Shitty analogy? You do better. You haven't been shot.

The agent. Gasping. "Sorry, ma'am. I had to."

He's hurt. I can see where I got him. There's an upper arm wound, looks to be an in-and-out, blood pulsing. I feel like that was the lucky second shot. The first shot is somewhere around his shoulder, and I realize he was wearing body armor, so it's taken most of the impact.

Davies. "To the car. Now."

We don't argue. We run back out toward the street. I hit the key fob to unlock the doors, hear them click. Isaac slides into the backseat. Davies, coming around the passenger side. Me behind the wheel. Doors aren't even closed before I turn the ignition and pull out, squealing the tires.

Cop car lights come around the corner as we're leaving.

CHAPTER 35

My arm throbbed with steady drum beats of pain by the time we made it to the interstate. The speedometer hovered around 80 as we barreled down the darkened highway. I eased up on the gas and took us down to 70. I debated on using cruise control. What were the rules for cruise control in the getaway from a death squad hit team? Is the term "death squad hit team" redundant. If you were a "death squad," I suspected you were by default also a "hit team."

Like the heat, blood loss does weird things to your thought process.

Davies rapped her knuckles against the passenger side window glass, watching the mile markers zoom by us. Isaac had his head slumped backwards, eyes closed, crying. The silence swallowed up everything else in the car.

"Are the police not going to be suspicious about the dead bodies they find all over the place?" I said. "We should have hung around."

"We couldn't take the chance," Davies said. "Sirens don't mean shit; it may have been anyone as far as we know." She sat up and turned on the cool, professional Davies. "I need to call in. Someone in the office needs to know."

"Like who? Because whoever organized the little hunting party on your not-so-safe safe house has turned agents." I checked my arm. The bleeding had slowed to a trickle. I'd most likely live from this. Lucky me. "It's good your guys are worse shots than Imperial stormtroopers."

"Find me a payphone," Davies said. "I can call Burwell."

"What about your cell phone?"

"I don't trust it. If they've gotten to field agents, then they may have gotten to our tech crews and might monitor calls."

I took an exit and pulled into a Sheetz parking lot. I parked in close to a bank of pay phones, underneath the humming buzz of the sodium vapor lights.

Isaac said, "I need to piss."

Davies said, "Go in with him."

"I doubt he needs me to hold it for him," I said.

"No, but take a moment to clean up your arm before it gets infected."

The woman had a point.

Inside the convenience store was almost an amusement park for sensory overload. A Katy Perry song blasted over the speakers. My ears rang with the sound of gunfire, and the music blurred with the ringing and the humming of the overhead lights. Two teenagers ordered a sandwich from the electronic kiosk. A skinny guy in overalls paid for a case of beer at the register. Kids loitered at the candy bars, and one slipped a Snickers into his shorts.

It was like those shitty movies schools used to show, telling you to stay off drugs. You know the ones, where one hit from a joint and the world shifts onto a 45-degree angle and everything turns into a collage of hysterical laughter, friends going out of focus, and calliope music everywhere.

We kept our heads down as rushed through to the store, pausing to grab bandages and peroxide before going into the bathroom.

It was 10 degrees colder than a meat locker in there, and reeked of bleach. The fluorescents reflected off the freshly mopped floors, but still managed to be darker than a bathroom needed to be. Do you need romantic ambiance when you were trying to drop a deuce?

Isaac stood at an urinal and started his business. I leaned against the sink counter and checked myself in the mirror. Blood covered the arm of my shirt, and I wasn't sure how much of it was mine. I pulled the shirt off and twisted around to get a better look in the mirror. The skin was jagged and raw and thick with clotted blood. I washed it using the pink hand soap from the dispenser, trying to be delicate and failing.

Then came the peroxide. I gritted my teeth as I poured it. It bubbled and hissed and ran down my arm in pink dribbles and burned like a motherfucker. My throat went tight, and I shut my eyes and I pounded at the sink counter. I waited a second, then gave myself another dose.

I burped, and all I got for the effort was bile and stomach acid. I was sure I would vomit. I knew that sensation. We had become familiar with one another, me and that knowing when I'm close to spewing out my insides, and I didn't like it. I also didn't care for how regular violence seemed, or how violence and vomiting had become linked for me. I wondered what would happen if I reached that point where something like this happened and I didn't care, that I didn't have a visceral response. Oh, just another day in my life.

Behind me, someone said, "You okay?"

I opened my eyes. Isaac watched my reflection in the mirror.

"Perfection," I said. "Can't you tell?"

He motioned toward my arm. "How bad is it?"

I shrugged. Big motherfucking mistake, since it pulled at the muscle close to where the bullet had passed. The sudden bolt of pain washed the world out into nothing but white and blood emptied from my head. My knees buckled. I braced myself against the edge of the sink, digging the heels of my palms in for support, and gave my head a good shake and sucked in some air, working to keep myself on my feet.

Isaac reached for me. I pushed back at him.

"I got this," I said, and blinked away until everything focused again.

With the blood washed away, I saw the wound was larger than I'd thought. They don't sell Band-Aid big enough to cover this.

I handed Isaac the box of bandages I'd brought in with me and told him to get me a roll of duct tape. Before he could say anything, I said, "Just do it."

When he came back with the tape, I ripped off inch-long pieces and stuck them on a paper towel. I pulled in all the air my lungs could hold and pinched together the skin on the wound.

I don't remember the shooting that ended my career with the state police; that has somehow been laundered and bleached clean from my mind. I don't remember getting my finger hacked off with pruning clippers. Your brain will shut down for these things, render those horrors unreadable in the memory banks. It's for your own well-being, so you can sleep at night, so you can function, so you don't turn into a drooling lunatic, forever caught in the Mobius strip of replaying your waking nightmares.

This pain, however, I don't think I'll ever be fortunate enough to forget. This pain was spectacular. It revitalized long-dormant neurons just to ensure I felt every mind-numbing, teeth-grinding, balls-shriveling piece of hurt.

In that moment, I loathed every member of my bloodline. I hated every failed condom, every missed birth control pill, every overlooked ovulation, every drunken hookup, every half-hearted 2 a.m. fucking, clocking back multiple generations, before the time one of my ancestors had come to America because he couldn't fucking grow potatoes in Ireland. Every thought, action or decision leading to my conception, my birth, and to that moment, I hated with a passion I'd never imagined possible. I wished a pox upon each and every filthy Mick born with the surname "Malone." That was how much it hurt.

I gave myself what felt like days to let the sensation pass. It was maybe five seconds, tops. Long enough to leave my face soaked in sweat, like I'd come out of a cold shower.

To Isaac, I said, "I need you to help me tape this closed."

His eyes swelled to globes.

I exhaled a little. "This isn't rocket science. Grab the tape and where I've got the wound pinched together, pull the tape over it."

"Don't you need stitches?"

"Yes, but unless we run across a doctor buying a meatball sub, this will have to suffice."

There are damn few things more redneck than using duct tape to suture a bullet wound. It was uglier than homemade sin on a Saturday night. I checked it out in the mirror, and it was a goddamn shit-show, but at least I wasn't still bleeding everywhere, which was all I could ask for.

Oh, and the fucking thing hurt. My brain adjusted to the pain, accepted this was the situation, and shut down enough so I didn't puke or pass out. It was the biggest favor the bastard had done for me since I was 12 and let me store away images of Penthouse centerfolds for later use.

We walked back out into the convenience store. No one gave us a second glance. Not much phases you at a convenience store in the middle of the night. I'd discovered as a state trooper, if you were out and about after midnight, you were headed somewhere, running from something, or looking for something. None of these are ever good when they're happening under moonlight.

I paid for what we had used, the cashier never looking up at me as he rang the items through. Outside, I saw Davies back at her car, standing with someone else I couldn't identify. As we got closer, I saw it was Burwell. They were talking, or least he was, while she looked tight-lipped and upset.

I said, "So has Agent Davies told you about our night?"

Burrell turned and pointed a pistol at me.

"Our night, which has gotten much worse," I said.

"Mine is a steam shovel full of shit itself," he said.

CHAPTER 36

"You could fuck up a wet dream, Malone," Burwell said.

Burwell sat looking somewhere between pissed and smug in the passenger seat of Davies' VW, his gun pointed at me. He had shoved Burwell into the backseat with Isaac, cuffing their hands behind their backs. Burwell cuffed me to the steering wheel. The asshole came prepared. No one had that many sets of handcuffs without also having a dominatrix on speed dial.

He made us toss our cell phones into the garbage back at the Sheetz. He didn't care I had eight months left on my contract. I guessed he didn't expect me to be around to close it out.

"I'm not sure how you guys are alive," he said. "They said they were sending eight guys in. In fact, when they told me the plan, I said it was too much. I already had a guy inside, so rein it in, I said. Nah, they said. Had to be sure. Be thorough."

"Always plan for contingencies," I said. "The cartels do not play."

"Which is now a problem I have to fucking deal with because of you ass swipes." He sighed. "Would have been considerate of you to just have killed Mathers. Now I have to do it before he sells my shit out, and that's compounded with getting rid of the ass bandit in the back seat."

Isaac said, "Fuck you."

Davies kneed the back of the seat. "Good agents died there tonight because of you, Lance."

I laughed. Burwell knocked me in the shoulder with the butt of his gun. "You think dead agents is funny?"

"No, but your name being is 'Lance' sure as fuck is," I said. "Did your parents intend for you to take the pork sword from birth, or assume that you'd back your way into it one day?"

He hit me, popping the pistol butt against the back of my skull. My head jerked, and I lost my focus and cut the wheel, and we swerved. I straightened the steering up, but the tires squealed, and I heard Davies and Isaac bounce around in what there was of the backseat.

"Watch what the fuck you're doing over there," Burwell said.

"Stop hitting me with that goddamn gun," I said.

Davies shook her head. "I got those tires a month ago."

Burwell rubbed his eyes with the palms of his hands. "You people. Jesus. There was a goddamn plan. The Mexicans would grab the faggot and go. Wait a few weeks, and someone would call in finding a body in a shallow grave, and it would get ID'd as Martin. Case closed, end of motherfucking story." He shook his head. "What the hell is it with you assholes fucking up a good plan?" He shot me an angry glare. "Especially you. If that big queen ex-trooper hadn't gotten slit open, no one would have given two shits about the bottom boy in back."

"Seems like an awful lot of people care about him now," I said.

"Yeah, seems that way." Burwell gave a casual shrug. "None of that is my thing. All I know is the boys in Juarez want him, and they seemed willing to write a big, fat nice check to make sure they got him."

From the backseat, Davies stirred around. "What about Price and Kaur then? Why kill them?"

Burwell wrenched his frame around to peer into the backseat. "I'm sure it will disappoint you that the people paying me don't keep me up to date on every bowel movement they make, or on why they opt to do certain things. They say 'frog' and I ask 'How high?'" A smile flickered across his face. "Goddamn but what a way to go out. These Mexicans are primal motherfuckers. They'll just blow your ass up, fucking Scarface-style." He made a motion with his hands like an explosion. "Ka-fucking-boom. Which makes how Price bought it even more pathetic. A bullet through the head? It's almost 'so what?'" He motioned with the gun toward the road. "You'll take an exit up here in a few miles, and I'll tell you where to go then."

If I had to guess, I figured his directions would lead to an abandoned field, desolate and away from anything. Somewhere to dump the bodies where they wouldn't be found for a while. By the time animals and the elements had had their way with us, an open casket would not be a possibility.

I glanced at Davies in the rearview mirror. She was thinking harder than I was. Thank God. I watched as she wiggled body around, pushing herself down in the seat. She saw me looking at her in the rearview mirror and jerked her head toward Burwell. Her eyes said Keep him busy.

My eyes responded, Got it. Or, at least I hoped they did. They're eyes; who knows what they said.

I cleared my throat. "They'll see you on the security cameras."

Burwell's attention had moved on elsewhere, his gaze on the window. He didn't even bother to look at me.

"Back at the gas station," I said, louder, pushing forward. "You're on whatever video surveillance system they've got at the gas station. Plus, there's a record of Davies calling you from a pay phone. They'll piece together your part in this."

Burwell leaned his head on the glass. "A fuck lot of good it'll do them. After I deliver McCoy, and I plan to vanish into the ether like a memory, somewhere without an extradition treaty with the U.S. of A." He pointed the pistol at me. "How much do you think a pound of twenties is worth?"

"No idea. Never came up in casual conversation."

"Nine thousand, eighty dollars. A pound of fifties is more than twenty grand. Twenty-two thousand, six hundred and fifty bucks. This is how those boys in Juarez count their money.

They weigh it because counting it takes too much time. Can you even comprehend that money?" He pounded the butt of the gun into his sternum. "I, meanwhile, drive an eight-year-old Honda with two bald tires. Why? Because I don't make shit, taking part in a fight I don't believe in, because how is selling drugs to the folks who want to use them the worst thing in the world? If nothing else, it's social Darwinism. Take out the weak ones, let the smart and strong survive."

"Which one are you, then?"

"Motherfucker, I'm mad-dog strong." He pointed at an exit sign. "Take that exit, then turn right."

We lost the freeway lights as we hit a county road. The interior of the car went black, the only light coming from the full moon, tinging everything in purple, making it feel otherworldly.

At the stop sign, I flipped a signal for my turn. Not like there was another car anywhere nearby. A courteous driver to the end. We passed the occasional house, a doublewide sitting off by itself on the side of the road, but otherwise, it was only us.

In the backseat, I saw Davies pushing herself further and further down. Her body was U-shaped by this point, knees high in the air, even with her head. Which was how most people sat in the backseat of a Volkswagen Beetle, I believe.

Burrell pointed to a narrow road on the left. "Head up that way."

I did as directed. I said, "Do you think you're so smart and important, the Mexicans will hand you a sack of cash and let you walk away? You don't think they'll just chop you into tiny pieces once you've done what they need done?"

Burwell let the pistol barrel swing toward my head. Even in the darkness, it's almost impossible to not know when there's a gun pointed in your face.

"You talk too fucking much, you know?" he said.

"So people tell me when I shut up long enough to let them talk." The words rolled out of my mouth strangled and forced. I tried to keep calm, to keep focused. I cleared my throat again, this time out of necessity. “Were you always this way?”

He chuckled. “What way are you talking about?”

“Selling out work, friends, colleagues, all for a few bucks.”

Burrell turned toward me. “Trust me when I say this is a lot more than a few—”

That was when he saw how Davies had shifted her body until her shoulders were flat on the seat and her legs were bent and in the air. Burwell tilted his head as he watched her pause for a second.

“What the hell—”

Davies kicked Burwell in the face. The crack of his nose shattering filled the car interior. He screamed out a muffled cry as blood gushed like a fountain. He aimed the gun toward Davies.

I braced myself, stiff-armed the steering wheel, and pounded the brakes. The car jolted and slid on the gravel, and we all flew forward. Burwell took it the hardest, his head smashing into the windshield, his body bending into something awkward and painful. The windshield spider-webbed from the blow of Burwell’s head. He grunted and folded like a lawn chair and slid into the floorboard. His pistol fired, the shot popping a hole through the roof.

Davies threw herself forward, wiggling between the seats. Burwell grunted and tried to lift his gun hand. Blood smeared across his face like war paint, and his nose didn’t look like a nose anymore, but hung limp off of his face, dangling like a piece of meat. Davies rammed a knee into his chest, her other leg pinning his arm against the console. He screamed and got off another shot that whizzed by my ear and cut through the headrest and shattered the back window. Isaac ducked into the seat.

Davies brought her knee up against Burwell’s jaw, over and over, each time banging his head against the glove compartment. He tried to scream, but it came out as a wet gurgling sound, and she jammed her knee harder, and Burwell’s teeth crunched, followed by something that sounded like a hunk of meat being cleaved, and fresh blood flowed from between his lips.

Davies pressed harder on his arm with her left knee and his hand fell limp and the gun dropped. She angled her leg against his throat and twisted her body around until she could reach the gearshift and put the car in Park.

She heaved a deep breath. Blood was everywhere.

"Fuck," she said. "And I got it detailed, too."

CHAPTER 37

Davies handed me the gun, told me to keep it on Burwell as she got out of the car, and pulled him out. She didn't try to be gentle, holding him by the lapels and yanking him free from the front seat floorboard. He collapsed onto the dirt into a sack of pathetic-ness, rolled his eyes upwards at up, and let his mouth drop open. Something fell out and landed in the dust. It was dark red and meaty. We all stared at it with equal parts bemusement, wonder, and disgust.

"That's what I'm thinking it is, isn't it?" I said.

Davies kicked at the chunk. "His tongue." The words came out with an off-handed casualness that would have made me laugh under almost any other set of circumstances.

Burwell mumbled something angry that didn't indicate he considered Davies funny. He had lost most of his fight and a substantial amount of blood. We cuffed his hands and feet together, shoved fast food napkins from the glove compartment up his nose to stem the bleeding, and propped him upright against the car.

I made tight circles with my wrists, getting the circulation going again. "I have to say, Davies, how you bent yourself in the backseat was impressive as hell. Saved our lives."

Davies cupped a hand around her eyes and peered into the car. "There are advantages to your girlfriend teaching yoga." She stood upright and stared at Burwell. "That's a horror movie.

How can one motherfucker bleed so much?"

Burwell sobbed a sad little noise and knocked his head against the fender of the VW.

"The bullet holes are more of an issue," I said. "You can't Bondo those. The bigger matter at hand is the question of who is left in the Bureau you trust?"

"A few hours ago, the answer would have been this asshole." Davies kicked at Burwell. Burwell sunk his head between his shoulders and stared at his feet. "Eleven months working with this fucker. Putting up with his shitty jokes and Vienna sausages for lunch and acting like he's got so much to teach me, and how I ought to be grateful to learn from him. Nearly a whole goddamn year of trusting him. Been to his goddamn house. Met his wife and kids. And he would have let me die out here."

"I doubt the plan was letting us die so much as killing us outright and leaving us to rot. They named his price right. Let's find somewhere safe and then you beat the mortal fuck out of him then."

Davies checked her watch. "Two-oh-four in the morning. I can call people in D.C., but I need somewhere to call them, and a place to hide until they can get us and Burwell."

Woody's place passed through my mind for a hot second. It made sense strategically, with as little as I knew about strategy. We'd be well armed if the Mexicans found us again. But there was still only three of us, and only two of us knew how to shoot a gun, and only one of us had a skill level that exceeded the zombie video game-level head-explosion lucky shot.

And while I worried about the Mexicans, I knew the Japanese also seemed an issue. Sure, they hadn't blown up anyone, but they didn't have issue throwing muscle around. They could have been coming after us also, and I wasn't sure even Woody had guns enough to help us fight off two competing sets of killers. I mean, okay, sure, he has more than enough guns, but those alone wouldn't keep us from getting killed. Plus, if anything happened to his dogs, it might be better to let a competing death squad kill me.

It was an exciting time to be alive. I hoped I got to be alive a little while longer to appreciate it all.

Isaac said, "Daddy's farm."

"What?" I said.

"The farm," he said. "My daddy's farm."

Davies smiled. "Funny. Okay, why not? Wait, and I'll tell you why not. Because it's a goddamn marijuana farm under so many government radars they could track Santa Claus for real, and it'll be the first place the Juarez cartel comes looking. Then the three of us go rolling in at two in the morning? No way. Much like Helen Keller, I do not see it happening."

"Honestly, not the worst plan I've ever heard," I said.

"Sweet Jesus, I hate to think what the worst was then."

"Is the farm still under surveillance?" I said. "If it is, then if there's anything that resembles trouble, they'll send people in, right? The jack-booted thugs those talk radio guys go on about will show up and save us. It'll be great."

Davies sighed. "We pulled back the surveillance once we brought Isaac in. It was part of the agreement when Isaac came into the system.

"Daddy's fortified the entire property," Isaac said. "There're tripwires and booby traps and electronic surveillance. My father used drones before the government thought about it. We're not counting how everyone there is my family, and everyone there has a gun within arm's reach. If you want somewhere safe, Agent Davies, I can't think of somewhere safer."

I looked at Davies. "What he said," I said.

Isaac stood up and dusted himself off. "Daddy installed his own cell phone tower years ago. The signal's impossible to track."

Davies shook her head. "Gonna be great when I call from there. I'll pile that onto the other shit to explain from tonight." She looked down at Burwell. "What about him?"

"We put him in the trunk, take him with us," I said.

"Seems like that would be awfully uncomfortable."

"Of the things in my world I'm worried about, his comfort level sits low on the list. Hell, I might hit a few potholes along the way."

"Might as well bust up the suspension while we're at it. Help me haul the fucker in there, then."

I considered shooting Burwell in the face. The moment happened while we moved him, and he tried to fight up some. I reached for the gun I had shoved in the back of my pants, which cooled his jets, and he stopping with the struggle. But I didn't let go of the gun, and I kept a thin-slitted gaze on him I didn't break.

It wasn't right, but that didn't matter. As I stared at him in the car's trunk, all I saw was his willingness to kill Isaac and Davies and myself, to sell out himself and his country for a few bucks.

He wasn't wrong on the drug stuff; this was fighting a war we didn't have a chance of winning, and arresting low-level dealers and users didn't solve the problem.

But I didn't buy that Burwell did what he did because he was following his beliefs. His speech was nothing more than his excuse to justify a desire for a paycheck, the words of a pissed-off man tired of seeing everyone with more than what he had, and wanting his share. His idea of the American Dream. Or he was just an asshole, and I could save us all a lot of time and kill him now.

Except I'd already shot one person in the head that night, which seemed like more than enough.

Davies looked at her former partner. I had my hand on the trunk lid, ready to close him up.

"I'll take Burwell in, and he'll answer for this shit," she said.

"You think he'll talk?" I said.

Burwell pushed his eyebrows together. It cracked the dried blood all across his face. He mumbled and made noises likely meant to be curse words, but instead came out as a meaningless jumble of wet sounds.

"Well," she said, "he'll try to. I guess he'll just have to write it all out."

Burwell drew back his lips and showed us his teeth, crusted in blood. "'Uck Ooo!" he said.

I shut the trunk lid.

CHAPTER 38

Isaac told us to stop so he could use a pay phone and call ahead to warn everyone we were coming. Davies said it was a bad idea.

"Showing up unannounced at this time of night is an even worse idea," Isaac said.

Isaac made his call, and we traversed our way through the many paths that took us to the McCoy farm. As we got closer, the gates opened to let us through, closing the moment we were clear.

Floodlights bright enough to illuminate a football stadium came on as we approached the farm. By the time my eyes had adjusted to the light, people were waiting for us. I counted close to a dozen, men and women, the youngest one a girl maybe 10, wearing a nightgown and holding a shotgun twice her size, the oldest a woman at least 80, a dried apple doll of a human being, carrying a semiautomatic rifle that seemed like it should have weighed enough to topple her over.

Tennis McCoy, in faded blue jeans and a denim shirt, his cowboy hat with its feather tilted to the back of his head, stepped out from the group and into the beams of the Beetle's headlights, hands in his pockets. He was the only person without a weapon.

I turned off the car's engine and got out. A few people lifted their weapons. Hammers cocked on guns. I kept my hands visible and a smile on my face.

"Morning, everyone." I said.

Tennis McCoy smiled. "Morning. I understand Isaac's with you."

"That he is."

"Then do you mind letting him out of the car? He's a tall boy, and I bet he's cramped up back there."

Wait until you check out what we've got going on in the trunk then, I thought, before I reached down and pulled the seat forward and Isaac climbed out. The smile on the old man's face grew wider as Isaac got closer, and he threw himself around his son, and Isaac pulled himself even closer to his father.

"I never thought you'd be back here," Tennis McCoy said.

"Neither did I, Daddy," Isaac said. He looked around his father to the armed individuals staring at us. "Granny? How're you?"

The dried apple doll said, "I'm doin' all right, Isaac. Glad to see you home. Your daddy, he said you were workin' for the government." She shook her head. "Don't see no need for such things. You ought just to come on back home." She looked at me. "This that boyfriend of yours I heard talk about?"

"No, ma'am. This is Henry. Pete—" Isaac swallowed hard, and his eyes glisten under the floodlights. "Someone killed Pete. Henry, he knew Pete, though. They were friends."

The old woman let her weapon drop to her side and she walked toward me. She gave me an up-and-down. "You a homosexual like Isaac?"

I shook my head. "I am not."

She looked at Davies. "This here your woman?"

I shook my head again. "She isn't."

Davies smiled and shrugged and said, "I am a homosexual."

The old woman looked taken aback for a moment. "Are you now?" She smiled, pulling back thin lips to reveal an oversized set of gleaming white dentures. "You're quite the thing then. Me, when all the boys left for the war, I had me a girlfriend or two. One of 'em looked a bit like you."

Tennis McCoy said, "Mama, this is not the time for this."

She shot an angry look back at her son. "You mind your manners, young man. This talk isn't about you." She turned her attention back to Davies. "You got yourself a woman?"

Davies said, "I do, ma'am."

The old woman lifted her shoulders. "Oh well. Your loss, honey." She turned to Tennis McCoy. "We should get them inside, get 'em fed. I bet they're hungry as hell."

"It's the middle of the night, Mama," Tennis McCoy said.

"Hunger don't give two damns about a clock," she said, heading off to the house. "I'll fry up bacon and potatoes. If any of you are hungry, it'll be ready right soon."

As she walked away, Tennis McCoy smiled at us with an expression in his eyes that pleaded for understanding.

"I hope to get old enough, I don't have to give a shit anymore," I said.

To Isaac, Tennis McCoy said, "The government coming to fetch you?"

Davies said, "That's what I'm hoping for. I need to make some calls, and I need to be somewhere safe to do it."

"This is about as safe of a place as you're likely to find," Tennis said. "That said, if it's all the same to you, I'd prefer the government not come here." He looked at Isaac, fatherly love all over his face. "What we do here, it's not legal by the definition of the government, but I'm still proud of Isaac here, having the courage to stand up and do the right thing here." He smiled at Davies and me. "I don't like the way those cartels do things. They hurt too many people. There's too much bloodshed, and that's a bad way to do business."

We showed Tennis McCoy the contents of the VW's trunk. Burwell bounced back and forth, screaming, the noise a guttural growl far removed from actual human speech.

To Davies, Tennis McCoy said, "This is your coworker, isn't it?"

"He was," she said. "We've severed our working relationship."

"He severed a chunk of his tongue while he was at it," I said.

"We didn't intend for that," Davies said. "Shit happened in the course of him trying to kill us."

"Nasty business," Tennis McCoy said. "Person like him, we should just feed him to the hogs."

The roar that emerged from Burwell was clean and nasty and pushed my hair back. Tennis McCoy shut the trunk lid, and Burwell's cries were muffled but no less noticeable as the tail end of the VW rocked back and forth.

"He's gonna shit his pants, isn't he?" Davies said.

"Quite likely," I said.

She sighed. "I almost had the goddamn car paid off, too."

CHAPTER 39

Grandma McCoy made a coffee that would have stripped paint off of wood. It made a chunky noise as she poured it from the pot. I stared into its inky blackness and expected something to stare back at me. It was a dark and empty void from which there was no escape.

Woody would have said it was weak.

Davies and I sat at the kitchen table while Tennis and Isaac had disappeared to elsewhere in the house. The table was set with ancient chipped plates and silverware at every chair, as if it was normal to have everyone up to eat in the middle of the night. Grandma McCoy fried up food sufficient to feed an infantry, scooping out spoonfuls of something thick and gelatinous from a coffee can and throwing it into a cast-iron skillet and then tossing in thick onion slices and slabs of potatoes.

The smell sent me back to being three and watching my mother make breakfast on weekends for Billy. It was one of the few solid memories I had of my mother. Most things about her were fuzzy and abstract, like modern art and the appeal of German hard rock.

But I remembered her dancing around the kitchen, Billy's stereo playing from the other room, Janis Joplin or Neil Young, while she chain-smoked her way through the preparations of eggs, sausages, and pancakes. Billy would spend the early hours in the garage, working on some beater he'd brought home like a stray dog, and come in with grease smeared across him, chasing her around the kitchen, trying to kiss her. She laughed and had none of that, tell him clean up before he could eat. We'd sit around the table and eat and laugh, and there was a legitimate happiness that would never be found again once she was gone. Breakfasts became another bowl of cold cereal, and Billy in the other room watching the morning news, seeming to count the seconds before I caught the bus and he didn't need to look at me and be reminded of the wife he had lost.

A radio from the back of the stove pumped out a gospel station on a signal so filled with static it might have been from Mars. It played an old-school hymn about the blood of Christ, sung in what should have been four-part harmony but sounded like four folks who were each out for their own interests.

Grandma McCoy stirred the potatoes around with a spatula, flipped bacon and sausage in another skillet, and joined in on the chorus.

Davies leaned into me. "What's she cooking those potatoes in?"

"My guess would be bacon grease," I said.

Davies looked at me like I'd spoiled a movie for her. "Who does that? Which should you worry about first: the salmonella or the cholesterol?"

Grandma McCoy smiled at us. I raised my coffee cup in her direction, and she turned her attention back to her cooking.

I sipped at my coffee. "I'll place a bet the old woman's eaten this way every day of her life, and there's a splendid chance of her outliving either of us," I said.

"But I don't eat red meat."

"And I don't eat pork. It's not eating bacon so much as just the grease. But she seems rather sweet on you, so I'm sure if you tell her, she'll make you up something else."

Davies ran a hand over her hair. "Let's add the octogenarian to my other 99 problems."

"I'd say if she's only in her 80s, you're lucky." I finished my coffee. There was a clump of grounds at the bottom you could dump into a coffeemaker and run through for a respectable pot. I set the cup aside. "Back at your house, your partner—"

"Felicia."

"Felicia. When she came in, she didn't seem thrilled with me being there."

"You're an observant soul."

"I suppose me being a guy, that didn't matter much, huh?"

"That was more the problem than anything. Felicia and I met two years ago. She teaches phys ed at the high school, and she's in the closet so much as no one calls her a dyke to her face, but she's an unmarried 40-year-old woman who teaches gym and drives a Subaru. Our daughter Emmy is adopted. Felicia got her when Emmy was only a few weeks old, when Felicia had given up on dating, and she didn't expect me to show up in her life. We met when I got transferred out to Clarksburg and CJIS, and I was running laps at the track and she was there and one thing led to another and we had that lesbian second date where you rent a U-Haul truck."

"How are things?"

"It's not been perfect, but nothing ever is. We've worked through issues—hers and mine—and made it work."

"Until—"

She nodded. "There's an 'until.'"

"There's always an 'until.'"

"Until last year, when I was in Omaha on a training thing, and there was a guy—"

"Plot twist."

"Don't. I may start to like you as a human being, and I would hate for you to ruin it by being who you are. Anyway, I've plowed both sides of the field, so to speak, but 99 times out of a hundred, my preferences are female."

"But this was that hundredth time, I guess."

"In a way. Felicia and I had been arguing right before I left. Ignorant crap, like what color to paint the living room. It was the stupidest thing to fight about, because nothing like that matters, but we've been together so long, we're out of the sane shit to argue about, and that left us with the minutiae. So I'm in Omaha, which is bad enough, and I'm out of town and lonely and tired, and I go to the bar and have a drink."

"Mistake Number One."

"I lost count of the mistakes that night. Another agent from the training is there, we start talking, I keep drinking, I let my guard down, and he invites me up to his room." She shrugged. "One thing led to another, and—"

"And your field got plowed."

She nodded. "But here's where it gets bad. I don't know what happened, because I had my phone in my back pocket and I must have butt-dialed, because I called Felicia as he and I were tearing clothes off one another."

"This wasn't one of those points where the call went to voicemail, was it?"

"Jesus but I almost wish. Felicia picked up her phone, and all she heard was—"

"The plowing of your field."

"Which, if I'm honest here, and I feel I can be since we've been in a shootout together, was an intense plowing."

"Loud, too, I bet."

"Very. This is a complete guy porn fantasy, isn't it?"

"I'm sure his letter to *Penthouse Forum* started, 'I didn't think these things really happened, but I was in Omaha—'"

"Things so rarely happen in Omaha. Felicia heard the whole goddamn thing. Which, when things calmed down a little, she said didn't sound like much compared to her and me, which I think was mostly to needle at me."

"Therein lies the eternal divide between men and women. You can marathon, and we're running a 5K."

"Some of you all can't break the tape on a 100-yard dash."

"I'm defending an entire gender here; cut me an amount of slack."

"'Slack' is usually the problem with men."

"Okay, I'm getting the point."

"Right, but we're wanting to get the point."

"Christ, but I'm just feeding you setups, aren't I?"

Davies laughed, but it didn't last long, and her voice turned pinched and pained. "It's been tough ever since. I didn't realize what happened until she called me the next morning, and she was in tears. Most people would have kicked my ass to the curb. Not Felicia; she's different. She loves me, and she said it hadn't been easy to get to where she trusted me again, because someone had screwed her over so many times before. Plus, there is Emmy, who loves me too, and I love her."

"But seeing a man in the house, one she wasn't expecting, that was a trigger," I said.

"She doesn't trust men. Or rather, she doesn't trust me around men. Which is funny, because I don't think I could cheat with another woman. There's not another woman who compares to Felicia. And neither do most men."

"Now she's suspicious and you carry guilt around."

"Both. Nonstop."

"What you have to accept is that you fucked up," I said. "We all fuck up. She's giving you a second chance. Be sure to take it."

"I didn't think about that when we fought tonight. I stormed out of the house—as much as you can without waking up a sleeping four-year-old, that is."

"And you called me."

"I did."

"Which saved Isaac's life."

"Seems that way."

"Then be grateful for that. We make it to the morning, you can work out everything with Felicia."

I refilled my coffee cup at the stove. Grandma McCoy added fresh strips of bacon to the skillet. She had fried enough to make two layers in a plate large enough to use as second base.

She brought a pan of biscuits out of the oven. They were perfect: golden brown, plenty of butter melted into the crust, big as a cat's head. She set them on the stove atop an unused burner.

As I looked at the food, my stomach did an involuntary growl.

"Be just a few minutes," Grandma McCoy said. "You keep yourself a seat at the table."

"Yes, ma'am."

Tennis McCoy and Isaac walked into the room. Davies came to her feet.

"Mr. McCoy, I need to make those calls so we can take Isaac somewhere safe," she said.

Isaac wouldn't look at us. He kept his head down, like we caught him in the midst of prayer.

Tennis McCoy took his hat off. He was bald, and his tanned scalp, marked by age spots, shined in the overhead kitchen light.

"I can't let that happen, Agent Davies," he said. "Isaac's not leaving with you folks."

CHAPTER 40

"Excuse me?" Davies said.

Tennis looked at Isaac. Tennis' expression was soft and caring, and he wrapped an arm around his son.

"I know the people coming after Isaac," he said. "They are among the nastiest people I've met, and I've dealt with many unsavory sorts. They'll get out of him what they want, and then they'll kill him. And you know as well as I do, they won't just put a bullet in his head. They'll make him suffer."

Davies knotted her hands together. "Mr. McCoy, Isaac is crucial to a federal operation."

"And Isaac is crucial to my heart." He pulled Isaac closer to him. "This is my son. And based on what you all have told me about tonight, I question the government's ability to keep him safe."

"You think you can?"

"It's a matter of Isaac not showing back up. You already have this computer thing, this Cashbyte, correct? I'm not sure there's more need for Isaac. Let me hide him away from these people." To Isaac, he said, "Sit down, son."

Isaac lowered himself into a chair at the table. Tennis poured himself a cup of coffee.

Davies crouched down in front of Isaac. "Talk to me. What is it you want to do here?"

Isaac sniffled a few times, worked to push back what would

grow into tears with little work.

"Think of Pete," I said.

Davies and Tennis both looked at me. They seemed surprised I'd said anything. I was shocked myself.

"Pete came here looking for you, and he died because of that," I said.

Isaac turned at his father, this baleful expression on his face like a dog unsure if he'd be petted or struck.

"They'll kill you too, Isaac," Tennis said.

"No, they won't," I said. "The cartel didn't kill Pete, and neither did the Japanese. Your family did, and now they're ready to sell you to the highest bidder."

The silence that fell over the room could have injured a person. I shifted my body to put my back against a wall and to keep a view on the doorways into the kitchen.

Grandma McCoy clinched a fork in her arthritic hand. She was ready for action—slow, joint-popping action, but she'd shove that fork between my ribs without a second thought.

"Momma," Tennis McCoy said. His eyes stayed on me. "Turn off the bacon and go on. We've got everything. Tell everyone to stay put. We have matters to discuss here. Just us."

She did as asked with reluctance, and shuffled her way out of the kitchen with small, methodical steps that reminded me of a Carol Burnett sketch.

The expression on Tennis' face never changed. The ones on Davies and Isaac sure as hell did. They looked as if they had found Gwyneth Paltrow's head in a box.

To Davies, I said, "Remember what Burwell told us. He said all he needed to do was deliver Isaac to his bosses. Not that he needed to kill Isaac. Why was that?"

A little light of realization shined in Davies' eyes. "Cashbyte."

"Cashbyte is the perfect mechanism to launder drug money, which is why the Feds want it, and why the dealers want it, too. Whoever controls that code can control a giant leap in criminal activity."

"But that means keeping Isaac alive," Davies said. "They need Isaac to maintain the code, to keep it clean."

"Which was why they murdered Price and Kaur. Insurance against the other two creators altering or changing anything in the code."

"So at the safe house tonight—"

"They weren't there to kill Isaac; they were there to take him from the Feds. Burwell was in the pocket to the cartel, so leaves the old man here to work for the Japanese, I bet." I looked to Tennis. "Still doesn't explain Pete's murder."

Tennis ate a piece of bacon. This may as well have been any of the thousands of other breakfasts he had consumed over a long life. "You gonna accuse me of killing Mr. Calhoun?"

"I don't think you did it yourself. There's no shortage of folks around here willing to cut up a queer if Grandpa says to do so."

Isaac retched and gagged and let out a sound that wasn't crying so much as an emotional dry heave. He pounded a fist against the kitchen table, and the contents jumped and rattled.

Davies and I watched as Isaac sobbed and choked and slammed his fist onto the tabletop over and over. Tennis ate another piece of bacon.

"You're an old man who doesn't want to spend his last years fighting a losing battle with a drug cartel," I said. "My bet is they're making a push into your business, aren't they? The guy Kaur and Price mentioned—"

"Wakahisa," Davies said.

"Wakahisa has deep pockets. Plus, I bet he offered you reach into an international market, too. When did he show up?"

Tennis drank more coffee, keeping his eyes toward the floor.

"So which are you planning on doing, Tennis? Are you hiding Isaac from the Mexicans, or are you selling him to the Japanese? It's a bit of both, isn't it?"

Tennis' eyes scanned the room. Isaac rocked back and forth in his chair, not saying anything. Davies' view ping-ponged between Tennis and me. I kept my sight on the kitchen door and a quick escape.

"I would never harm my son or anyone close to him," he said.

"Unless it interfered with your business," I said. "Your family's reputation precedes you for dealing with competition."

"Boogeyman stories, that's all. People love to pass on these impossible tales. Besides, you saw me give Mr. Calhoun the money. Why would I kill him and steal the money back?"

The coot had me. Maybe he hadn't—

"How d'you know about the money?" I said.

Tennis raised his eyebrows. "What?"

"The money you gave Pete," I said. "How d'you know it was stolen?"

"What money?" Isaac said. The voice was small, but full, and surprising. His hands lay flat on the tabletop. He lifted his head and looked at Tennis.

"Your father gave Pete a hundred thousand dollars the day we came here," I said.

Tennis seemed smaller than he had a heartbeat prior. His body language screamed he had been caught. "Isaac, I did it because we couldn't tell him the truth."

"So somehow money would fix it?" Isaac said. "You thought paying him would solve the problem. Pete loved me, Daddy."

"Isaac, please—" He stepped toward his son.

"Stop right fucking there." Isaac's voice dripped venom and ice water. Tennis listened to his son's command. "Don't. Just. Don't." Isaac drew his lips into a tight bow. "You came and said you had an idea. Said it would help the family. Once I left here and made my own life, you said you had seen about cryptocurrencies on the news. Except you didn't call them that. You called them 'electronic money.' You said I could develop something like that."

"So Cashbyte was your idea," I said to Tennis. "Shame you never got to settle that pissing match between Kaur and Price."

Tennis stared at his son. "I was honest with you, Isaac. What you made, it will help the family. It takes the danger out of getting paid—"

I said. "Talk to me about the missing money, Tennis."

The old man turned to me. He didn't seem calm, bemused, or genteel anymore. He seemed like someone who had lost control of a situation, mired in a circumstance he was unsure how to navigate.

"Shut up," he said through gritted teeth.

I pushed on. What was there to lose?

"No one's said anything about that money. It wasn't in the newspapers, and the police aren't talking about it." To Davies, I said, "Did you tell Tennis about the money?"

Davies swallowed hard enough for it to be audible. "I didn't."

"The other one," Tennis said. "The one in the trunk. Burwell. He told me." His voice lacked the strength and authoritative nature it had before. He had a lot more quiver in it now.

"Right," Isaac said, nodding. He worked to hold back tears.

Davies said, "But I was at every meeting with you, Mr. McCoy, and Burwell never told you about the money when I was there."

Tennis said, "Woman, you need to shut your mouth."

"No, she doesn't," Isaac said. "You told me the Japanese would help me, that they'd hide me and keep me safe. You said you talked to Wakahisa, and he'd protect me. And what you're really doing is selling me to them."

Tennis breathed a sigh. "Isaac, understand this. This is bigger than you or me. This is for your family."

The fork was in Isaac's hand, and he leaped from the table and tackled his father. They were both on the ground, Isaac on top of Tennis, and Tennis never had time enough to scream before Isaac stabbed him in the neck. He repeated the action over and over, blood spurting in the air, splattering across Isaac's face, the sound of the fork tongs piercing flesh and sinew, then cracking the old man's trachea. Tennis' body spasmed, but not much, held down under Isaac's weight. Isaac raised the fork and plunged it over and over into his father's throat.

At first, it was like watching a horror film, one I couldn't turn off. Then the shock wore off, and Davies and I leapt forward and grabbed hold of Isaac and pulled him back and off his father's body.

Blood covered Isaac's face, so thick and dark the only other thing you could really see was the whites of his eyes. Those eyes had gone devoid of feeling, thought, care, concern, familial connection, or the acknowledgement he had just killed his father. He didn't even breathe hard. He seemed unaware of anything around him, existing only inside this moment, separate and alone from everything else.

I took the fork from Isaac's hand. He didn't put up a fight. I moved him into a chair. He stared blankly at me. Closer to through me.

To Davies, I said, "We've got to go."

Davies stared at Tennis' body. Blood pooled around him like a crimson halo.

"Now," she said. "We've got to go now."

CHAPTER 41

We weren't quite to Davies' car when there the sound of a shotgun getting racked behind us rattled through the night air, and someone said, "Hold it right there, fuckers."

I cranked my neck around to peek over my shoulder. Jed, the kid who'd met us on the four-wheeler during the first visit, had a shotgun in his hands. He chewed on a toothpick like he'd seen in a movie, trying to appear like a tough guy. Behind him stood two other boys. They had been staring down at us from windows up in the house the first time we had come out. They held rifles I couldn't identify in the darkness, but the bullets would hurt anyway.

"Which one of your fuckers did that to my grandpa?" Jed said. His voice came out as a cross between a hiss and a growl.

I said, "Why d'you pump the action on that shotgun?"

"What?"

I pivoted on my right foot, the foot shifting behind me, when Jed said, "I didn't say you could fucking move."

I glanced at Davies and Isaac. All I could see for the mess of the blood on Isaac were his tired eyes, defeated in the moonlight. Davies's mouth pulled tight and thin.

I lifted my hands into the air. "Can we turn around?"

"How come?" Jed said.

"Does it matter why? You guys are pointing the guns at us, not the other way around. I just don't want shot in the back."

Jed offered the question the consideration most people give ordering fast food, and said, "Go on."

I looked at Davies and Isaac. "Both of you, hands up. Fingers wide apart."

Davies looked as if the action caused physical pain. She raised her hands, every muscle and tendon stretching taut in the motion. Isaac did it quicker, sighing as he moved.

We each twisted ourselves around to face the trio. Jed glared at us. He gave Isaac a hard stare and shook his head and raised the shotgun into a firing position.

I took a half-step over, in front of Isaac. Jed watched at me from the far end of the weapon. I looked down the barrel. I didn't much care for the view.

Jed held steady with his aim. "Mister, this'll go through you as much as it'll go through him." He had one eye shut and a cold, solid hold on the weapon. "He's going down."

Jed was about 15 feet away. He kept the shotgun aimed chest-level on me. The spread on the shot from the weapon would tear me apart, spray chunks of me in every direction, shatter my bones and splatter my guts all over the place. It would kill Isaac, too, though he'd linger awhile since I'd have taken the biggest brunt of it. They might put a second shell in him, to put him out of his misery, or they might let him bleed out and die in agony, as their version of justice.

I did this entire calculation of pain and suffering in my head in the time it took to blink. A by-product of friendship with Woody was learning these sorts of things.

"You never answered my question," I said. "Why d'you rack the shotgun?"

Jed kept his bead on me, but his face shifted a little. You could almost sense the thoughts going through his head, the rattling of barely formed ideas knocking around an otherwise empty void.

"Got your fucking attention, didn't it, though?" he said.

"It did. You saw it in a movie, didn't you?"

More thinky-hurty expressions. Neurons that had laid

dormant for years fired to life, stretching out and clocking in for work.

"What if I did?" he said. "You got a fucking point, asshole?"

"It's a waste of a shell."

He opened both eyes and angled the barrel down to where it pointed in my stomach/crotch vicinity. I felt myself stop breathing for a moment, and I decided I would rather he shot me in the chest, all things being equal. I guess, however, that's not how it goes as far as getting shot-gunned goes.

He drew his finger away from the trigger. Air went out of my lungs. I smiled.

"You hadn't fired yet," I said. "You only need to pump the action on a shotgun after you've fired. Otherwise, you're wasting a shell. They do that all the time in movies, and I'm guilty of doing myself, but it's a bullshit kind of thing, something they do because it looks bad ass. Which it does, but if it comes down to matters of need, which would you prefer: to look badass, or to have the wasted shell?"

Jed sighed and raised the shotgun so the barrel stared down at Isaac and me.

"You fuckers are gonna die tonight," he said. "You gonna do this hard or easy?"

A figure walked toward us. It was Grandma McCoy. She came up behind her grandsons. They parted and let her through.

"Put the gun down, Jedidiah," she said.

Jed kept the shotgun raised.

"He killed Grandpa."

"Do as you're told."

There was a pause, and Jed lowered the gun.

Grandma McCoy walked over to Isaac. A painful smile pushed deep into her face.

"You did that, didn't you?" she said. "In the kitchen?"

Isaac nodded.

"What your friend said about your daddy, him killing your

man, that was true?"

Isaac nodded again.

Grandma McCoy shook her head.

"We didn't know," she said. "I didn't know, and I never would have let this be."

"I wouldn't suspect you would, Grandma," Isaac said. "There wasn't any good way for him to tell you."

She reached up and touched her grandson's face, covered in her son's blood. "Your daddy, he was a lot of things, but I don't suppose he was always an honorable man. He never seemed to get that family was all that mattered."

"Pete was my family, Grandma." Isaac bowed his head and cried. Grandma McCoy reached out and pulled him into her, resting his head on her shoulder. Isaac cried harder. She seemed oblivious to the blood that covered him. She patted him on his back, and leaned into his ear and sang so softly, I strained to hear.

"I'm just a poor wayfaring stranger
Traveling through this world of woe
There's no sickness, toil nor danger
In that fair land to which I go
I'm going home to see my father
I'm going home no more to roam
I'm just a-going over Jordan
I'm just a-going over home."

She sang without form or tune, in a voice no one would have mistaken as pretty, but that didn't matter. Nothing else mattered. It was a woman comforting her grandchild over a loss, a woman who'd lived a life filled with losses, and understood the pain.

Davies and I stood there, unable to say anything. No one else seemed able to, either. The moment was personal in a way that didn't let you comment, but just observe, because it didn't need us to make it about us.

When she finished, she took Isaac by the shoulders and pulled him back and righted him, gave him a slight shake.

"What your daddy did, that was wrong, no two ways around it," she said. "And you got angry and did what people would do. You lost your shit."

Jed moved towards them. "This faggot killed Grandpa, and we're supposed to just let him walk out?"

Grandma McCoy gave Jed a look that pushed him backwards without touching him. "You know the first goddamn thing about loss, Jedidiah McCoy? You've never been off this piece of land, doing nothing but killing things that didn't need killing, waiting on someone to die so you can get their share of whatever it is, doesn't matter if it's money or chicken gravy. I don't know you've ever loved nothing that wasn't your own dick, so don't be telling me or anyone else who's lost something how it is." She looked back at Isaac, her expression softer. "Isaac, he headed off into the world, found himself family, and he lost it."

She pushed herself around Isaac to see Davies. "Where you gonna take him now?"

"I'm not sure, ma'am," Davies said. "The DEA will still likely drop the investigation into your marijuana business, and Isaac may play a role in getting some dangerous people off of the streets."

"It's a damn shame to use people's loved ones against them," Grandma McCoy said. "Must be one reason we've stayed off to ourselves. Except Tennis; he always thought there was a need to keep getting more. He always wanted to make it bigger, make it bigger, didn't matter how many times I told him we done got everything we need, and we got everything we want, so what's 'more' than that?" She shook her head. "Damn child never listened, even as an old man."

She smiled at Isaac. "You go on now. We got stuff to clean up." A tear ran down her cheek, caught in the corner of her smile. "There's likely not much time left for me on this side of dirt. It will not be a good idea, you decide to show back up to the family reunion or my funeral, so this is gonna have to be the goodbye we get. You good with that?"

Isaac choked back a sob. "Thank you, Grandma."

She hugged him again. "You and these folks go on. The gentleman in the trunk, we done took care of him." There was a bend to her voice meant to imply humor. I suppressed a chill. "That blood, we couldn't do nothin' about, though." She smiled at Davies and winked. "Sorry about that, honey." To Jed, she said, "Get your ass into the shed, get out shovels, head back to the family plot, start digging the holes."

Holes, I thought. Plural. Eek.

They turned and walked away. No one said anything to us, or gave us a second glance, as we got into the VW, and drove away.

CHAPTER 42

Davies and I were at the lunch counter at the Riverside. I had a cheeseburger, and she picked at a salad that didn't seem to be much more than iceberg lettuce and radishes. I think I saw a sliver of tomato.

"Isaac's back to working on Cashbyte," she said. "We'll re-introduce it under a new name, create a fresh cover story for it. It won't be what we had hoped, but there's still something they can salvage from it."

"Anything said about Tennis?"

"Who's going to say what? Homicide is a local matter, and the McCoy family never reported a crime. The only reason we know Tennis McCoy is dead is because we watched it, and I'm sure as hell not going to say anything about it." She looked at me. "What about you?"

"I've got no reason to want to relive that slasher film of a night. This also negates a solution for Pete's murder. How did Tennis work the deal with the Japanese?"

"The best we put together was after Pete's murder, and there was a greater threat to Isaac, that opened the door to use their money and resources against the cartels muscling into his trade. When we hand-delivered him Isaac, it was exactly what he wanted."

"Would Tennis even thought of this if Woody and I hadn't shown up with Pete?"

Davies pushed lettuce around on her plate until the steel tongs scraped against the ceramic. I drank some iced tea and nodded my head.

"What you're saying to me by not saying anything is Woody and I helped Pete get killed," I said.

Davies pushed away the plate. "Don't do that, Henry. You'll lose your mind if you do. Who knows what would have happened. I think that little homophobic psycho Jed who was so intent on shooting us that night has a hundred grand hidden somewhere, and a lack of a conscience about what he did." She rested her elbows on the counter. "Tennis understood what giving the money to Pete would do to someone like Jed. He cocked the hammer on that and just waited."

"But we can't be sure of that."

"No, we can't. But what we can be sure of is Wakahisa was involved with people he shouldn't have been involved with because they found his body cut up into small pieces and shoved into several heavy-duty garbage bags on a curb in Pittsburgh. It took dental records and someone good with jigsaw puzzles to ID him."

"Obviously they weren't happy Wakahisa couldn't provide Isaac as promised."

"Obviously. About the only obvious thing is this whole goddamn mess. Otherwise it's just a litany of unanswered questions."

"Things don't always get tied up in a neat little bow, the way we want them to, do they?"

"My life is like that." Davies pushed her salad away. "You tell anyone about what happened?"

"Hell no. Who the fuck would I going to tell?"

Spoiler alert: I lied. I had told Woody while he was still laid in the hospital once he woke the hell up, sore and unhappy about his pickup. He listened to the story and told me I was the luckiest gimpy bastard alive.

After Davies, Isaac, and I cleared the McCoy farm, we drove

to Marlington and Davies called her contacts. The longest fucking hour of my life later, a series of anonymous black Ford SUVs pulled up, and guys in FBI jackets got out, and I half-expected someone to say, "Come with us if you want to live." It would have made my day if they had. They strapped bulletproof vests onto us and hurried us into the vehicles. The vests seemed rather "a day late and a dollar short," but as in so many situations, I doubted anyone cared what I thought.

Someone asked why Isaac was covered in blood. Davies and I said it was from the gunfight at the safe house. No one pushed for more on the answer.

They drove us to the Clarksburg FBI building and took us straight onto a helicopter and flew us somewhere that I was sure was Washington.

They interrogated me for hours, just to make sure I was as clueless as I seemed to be, and I tried to not disappoint. Everyone was firm but polite, and they kept asking me what I knew about Burwell's involvement in this cluster of fuckery. I told them I didn't have a clue, and they finally seemed to accept that, which was good since all I had to go with there was the truth.

I ate a French fry.

"How are you and Felicia?" I said.

"We're fine," Davies said. The tone didn't match the words.

"You know what 'fine' means in AA."

"Fucked up, insecure, neurotic, and egotistical."

"Want to reconsider your answer?"

"No. We're at where we're at for the time being."

"Still sleeping there?"

"Fitfully, but yes. Trust isn't the issue so much as—"

"The issue is the fact you almost died."

Davies nodded and wiped at the corner of her eyes. "It's tough to face how close she came to being a widow."

"Cops, Feds, anyone with a shield and a gun, they sign up aware of what it's like to deal with that. Divorce is an occupational hazard, but no one wants to give up the occupation."

Davies folded her hands on top of the table.

"Growing up gay, I never had this romantic idea of being married, because it's not what lesbians got to do. Other girls, they planned weddings and tried on dresses and made bridal registries and all of that. I wanted to find someone to grow old with, and we'd rescue huskies together. My life course, though, that was a definite. I always wanted to be a Fed. But when I met Felicia, she brought a family with her, ready-made, and I wasn't ready to give those things up, but I'm not ready to give up doing my job, either, so someone needs to explain why the hell I have to make that kind of choice."

"Things work out," I said. "We don't always like how they work, but they do. The only choice we've got in any of it is accepting it and moving forward and hoping to not fuck it up any further than what it is."

"Is this your idea of being comforting?"

"It's why I don't sponsor."

CHAPTER 43

The hospital kept Woody for a while, so I told him I'd keep an eye on the dogs for him. He didn't seem to trust the idea entirely, but that was because Woody doesn't trust anyone entirely.

The dogs gave me side-eye for the first day, but got used to me by the second. Since I had the run of Woody's place, I opted to make use of the freedom and spent time on his gun range. I worked my way through a variety of handguns, emptying clip after clip until my fillings wouldn't stop vibrating and the air stunk of gunpowder.

When I wasn't at Woody's, I busied myself keeping up with Jed McCoy.

I won't say Jed did much of anything interesting. He didn't seem to have a secret life, or much of a life period. He was a punk-ass 18-year-old who didn't come out of the holler much, but when he did, it was in a rusted-out pickup sitting on a jacked-up suspension with oversized tires.

He had a girlfriend. She was a chunky thing with a bad complexion, and she hadn't figured out the three things in life that always tell the truth are young children, drunks, and Spandex pants, and her Spandex pants did not say nice things about her. She lived a few miles from the McCoy farm, and Jed would pick her up and drive out to a nearby cemetery and they would do things in the back of the pickup that tested the truck's suspension and the realms of good taste.

Other times, he met with a group of kids who all looked his age and his IQ, and they'd jump onto four-wheelers and vanish up into the hills with rifles in tow, and come back down with a bunch of dead squirrels, or an out-of-season deer.

Every Sunday morning and every Sunday evening, he drove out to a small church with a dirt parking lot and signs that read "GOD SAID ADAM AND EVE, NOT ADAM AND STEVE" and "SATAN WAS THE FIRST TO DEMAND EQUAL RIGHTS". From a distance you could hear the clatter of gospel played on electric guitars and the preacher's roar as he assailed the sins of the world.

Yeah, I bet they were a bag full of laughs.

Sometimes I followed Jed in my Aztek, and other times I used Billy's pickup. Once, I borrowed a four-wheeler from one of Billy's neighbors. I tried to switch it up enough so Jed didn't catch on he was being watched. I'm not sure Jed would have figured it out. Nothing showed he was the sharpest pencil in the drawer.

On a Sunday night, he parked his truck toward the back of the church lot. I watched from a distance as the small crowd filtered in through the doors, and then the music shook the building to life.

I took a length of rubber hose and some gas cans and went to Jed's truck and siphoned fuel from the tank. Sucking on the hose, and the spew of gas that filled my mouth at first, almost made me puke, and I struggled to hold it back while I aimed the hose into one of the gas cans. I pulled gas from the tank until it wouldn't let me get anymore. Then I added back a smidge. Not much, though. I didn't need him to get very far; just away from the church. Away from people.

I hoped this would work. I'm not a mechanic or an engineer, and I wasn't sure what sort of fuel mileage a piece of shit like Jed's got. I knew what my piece of shit got, which sucked and kept me at the gas pumps, so I guessed and hoped I was right.

I made it back to my Aztek with the gas cans as the church

doors opened and the congregation emptied into the parking lot. I watched through night vision binoculars as Jed got into his truck and drove off.

I parked on a ridge that overlooked the church and gave me both an open view of the lot and a clear path to the main road. I let him a minute before I drove out and onto the road and headed in his direction. He had three or four minutes on me. I figured between fuel already in the engine, combined with the drops I'd put in his tank, he would at most get five or six miles down the road before the truck would sputter off and die.

For once in my life, I was not disappointed.

He had pulled the truck over off onto the side of the road with the flashers on. He had the hood up, and was bent over into the engine, poking around.

I pulled off just in front of him. Late at night, dark, and he didn't know my vehicle anyway, so he'd assume he was being saved by a Good Samaritan.

He turned as I approached him, smiling at first. The lights from the truck's headlamps caught my face about then. Recognition hit him like a hammer, and he saw the pistol in my hand, and he turned rabbit and tried to run.

I hit him with the Taser. The twin cable sprung forth from the device and caught him in the back, and the electrical jolts raced through the wires and turned him into a marionette at the end of a string, his body dancing and flailing like someone filled with the Holy Spirit, before collapsing limp onto the ground.

The reek of piss hit me as I got close to him. The wet stain at the front of his pants was unmistakable.

I held the chloroform-soaked rag over his face. He gave in without a fight, his body melting into dead weight. I dragged him over to the Aztek and loaded him into the back end and drove away.

***

Jedidiah McCoy woke up tied to a tree. It was a little after 10, and the only light in the woods came from the Aztek headlights.

I'd picked the spot because it was miles from the McCoy farm, and miles from my house. There were makeshift ATV trails of muddy ruts worn into the ground, but I didn't get the feeling this was a well-traveled area. Which was what I needed.

It hadn't been easy to stand him upright and get the ropes around him, but the look on his face when he woke up—the sheer and utter stark terror, frothing at the mouth and struggling against the ropes so hard it tore open his skin and blood dripped to the ground—made the work worthwhile.

I aimed the Taser at him again and said, "Cool your shit or else."

He had a moment where he considered resisting more, but it passed, and he slumped back into the tree.

I let a smile flicker across my face. I had made sure the ropes were tight, and I'd strapped his wrists to his thighs for extra measure, so I could get in close. And because there wasn't much he had to say I wanted to hear, I stuffed a sock in his mouth and wrapped duct tape around his head to keep it there.

I leaned in close to him. "You comfortable? Not that I give a fuck, but it seems the polite thing to ask."

He mumbled something angry.

I took a few steps back. "I'll ask you a question, and you'll answer. Don't make this more complicated than it is already. Did you kill my friend Pete?"

Jed tried to scream, but nothing came out. I hoped he was getting a mouthful of the sock; I'd worn it for a few days, and made it sure it got especially warm, wet, and ripe.

I fired the Taser. As soon as the metal barbs hit him in the midsection, Jed froze and stopped trying to talk. I didn't activate the device and kept my thumb on the button.

"It's a 'yes' or 'no' thing," I said. "Did you kill Pete?"

Jed's head rose and fell.

I sighed.

"I suppose that was the answer I expected. I thought you'd put up more of a fight, but you're such a proud yet ignorant bit of pig shit that confessing to murdering a cop doesn't bother you much does it?"

Jed said nothing. Technically, he couldn't, but he didn't even try, either. His eyes stayed wide and scared.

"You know, a while back, my friend Woody and I, we needed information from a guy—a hair or two older than you—so we took him and handcuffed him to a pole and did a redneck water-boarding on him. It was December, and he was naked, and he wasn't happy about it, but he put up a fight."

My thumb tapped the activation switch on the Taser. Jed's eyes met there, focused, waiting.

"The thing was, I don't know if he was a bad person," I said. "He was stupid as fuck, and he fell into a group that gave him something when he had nothing, but like I said, I don't know that he was a bad person. But the price he paid for being an idiot, for talking to me, was he got set on fire, and he got pissed on while he burned alive."

I stepped closer to Jed. "I need you to answer this question for me again, Jed. Did you kill Pete?"

It took a moment for the words to connect, before he nodded again.

I sighed. "I know without doubt you are a bad person. You're a lousy excuse for a human being. I am not sure why you killed Pete. If the old man told you to, or if you wanted the money he gave Pete, or you thought God spoke to you, or you like killing people. But whatever the reason was, it doesn't matter. What matters is you took someone away from someone else."

I took hold of the cables and gave a hard yank and pulled the barbs out of Jed's chest. The sock suppressed his scream, but make no mistake that his point was understood.

I said, "So you know, Jed, I debated on killing you. I thought long and hard about bringing you out here and putting a bullet in your head. It's the same debate I had with myself over wanting to kill Burwell. I didn't, though, because I was convinced there'd be justice. We'd take him to the authorities, and they would met out whatever was appropriate. Your kin took care of that, however, and I can't say his fate wasn't what he deserved.

"But I can't take you to the police. You confessing to me wouldn't be worth shit in a court. But you killing Pete, there's gotta be something for what you did."

I turned and paced off 20 steps, and bent down and picked up a handful of stones. One by one, I whizzed them toward the tree. Most missed Jed by a mile, but two or three nailed him. The fun part was watching him wince as they flew by his face, as he tried to dodge them and couldn't move.

I was toying with him. The cruel part of me wanted him to suffer. He deserved that, to be made to squirm and hurt. There weren't enough rocks or enough nighttime to make him feel what he had coming to him.

I heaved a breath. I couldn't push this all night. I didn't have the bit of heartlessness that Woody had, the ability to separate from my actions on an emotional level.

Jed stood there, breathing hard, crying.

I said, "I won't kill you, Jed. As much as you deserve to die, you're not worth the nightmares I'll have."

Relief swam across his face. He cried harder, but it took a distinct tone, filled with gratitude.

"But—" I said.

The noises stopped, and his body locked tight again.

"I'm not letting you go," I said. "I'm leaving you here. My guess is we're six or seven miles away from anything like a road. You might work your way out of those ropes, then bumble your way to the road, and then find a way home. No idea how long it'll take you, but it'll be interesting to find out."

Jed lost control of everything inside him. He screamed and cried and tried to struggle his way out of the ropes, and he only ripped himself open more.

I watched him until he wore himself out, and then I said,

"One last thing: should you get out of there, and if I ever, for any reason, see you again, that is when I'll kill you. Don't have revenge in your heart or think you need an eye for an eye, because I will put you in the ground myself. And if you're lucky, and you get me first, trust me that my friend Woody will come for you, and he's not as nice of a guy as I am."

I got into the Aztek and drove away as Jed's muffled cries tries in vain to get through the night. As I drove further away, winding around until I found pavement and heading for home, I thought I could still hear him.

I turned on the Fleetwood Mac CD to drown it out.

CHAPTER 44

The paperwork from Maggie's attorney rested on the kitchen table, where I'd left it that morning, and every morning since I'd gotten it. It had been there so long, Izzy had stopped sniffing at it once we came inside, during her ritual pilfering for food crumbs she might have missed.

I started a pot of coffee. There was a knock at the door. It was Woody.

"How you doing, sport?" I said as he pushed past me.

"Great. Even better if you never call me 'sport' again."

Woody hobbled his way into the kitchen, using a cane to support himself. I had given him the name of my physical therapist and told him what an absolute delight she was. After the first appointment, he called and threatened to beat me to death with his cane.

He took a seat at the table.

"Still driving the rental from the insurance company?" I said.

"Yeah. Anonymous looking four-door something or another. Thing's got no style. I lose it every time I go to Wal-Mart, on account it looks like every other goddamn car in the parking lot. I can't find anything I like."

"I imagine you're going for something inconspicuous, like a 1955 Thunderbird. Aqua blue, maybe."

"If I continue to associate with you, I should get something bulletproof." He gave me an appraising look. "How you doing?"

I shrugged. “I’m okay.”

“Even about—”

“Yeah.”

“You think he got free? Think he’s alive?”

“I drove out there yesterday. The ropes were laying there on the ground. There was an awful lot of blood on them, and all around the tree. He paid a price for getting loose.”

“And if he comes looking for you?”

I sipped my coffee. “I guess I’ll kill him.”

“Very matter-of-fact of you.”

“I couldn’t justify killing him that night. I can justify it if he shows up one night uninvited.”

“Think you can handle doing that?”

“Under most circumstances I’d say ‘no, ’but for Jedidiah McCoy, I can make an exception.”

“Fair enough.”

Woody’s eyes went to the envelope on the table.

“I notice this is still here,” he said.

“It is.”

“It’s been here a while.”

“It has. Thanks for noticing.”

“You need to fucking fish or cut bait with this stuff, brother.”

“Her attorney’s saying the same thing.”

“Then what’s the wait? Besides you being an asshole.”

I poured us each some coffee and sat down at the table.

“I’m not ready.”

“How long is it going to take you to be ready?”

“However long it takes.”

“You talk to that principal anymore?”

I’d made the mistake of mentioning Dr. Wilder to Woody. I’d called her up, and we’d met for coffee, and she’d said things would go a lot more smoothly if I stopped calling her “Dr. Wilder” and called her “Lily.” I told her she was probably right.

“We’ve had dinner a few times,” I said. “Exchanged texts

and whatnot. We're remaining in our upright and seated positions, however, if that's what you're hinting at. I'm not in a rush, and neither is she."

Woody smiled from behind his coffee cup.

"It's time to move on, Henry."

"I know."

"Then what the hell's your problem?"

"I'm not ready."

Woody drank some coffee.

"You say you don't know anything about me, so here's this thing that happened," Woody said. "Three different energy conglomerates wanted to build this new oil pipeline in the Middle East, in one of those countries that end in '-stan'—I don't even remember which one it was anymore—but they couldn't because some dickhead had set himself up as the supreme ruler of about a hundred square miles of sand where this pipeline needed to go. He'd gotten himself some followers and some guns and control over a few villages and decided that no 'white devils' would build through his little kingdom because it was somehow sacred land.

"I suppose there was a way to have built around the hundred square miles of sand, but it would have been expensive, and the conglomerates weren't about to let this guy cut into their profit margins, so they decided it was cheaper to hire me to kill him. I got together a team of guys not afraid to get their hands dirty, and we found where he lived, planted C-4 everywhere, blew the thing all to motherfucking kingdom come. Which was great, except he wasn't there. We kill off three of his wives and most of his children. We send him a message to stand the fuck down, and he sent us back someone's finger. The middle one. That asshole, he wouldn't budge.

"Next we heard he was traveling with a convoy. Ten trucks, loaded to bear. My crew took the convoy out. Ten of us, and forty of them, but all anyone ever did was hand them automatic weapons and tell them how to pull the trigger and where to point. More C-4, Winchester Model 70 bolt actions with scopes, we picked 'em off until there were two left, and we marched in and killed one of them and found the last person alive was the warlord's 13-year-old son. That little fucker pulled a gun and shot one of my guys in the chest. The body armor caught the shot, but my guy killed the kid.

"The warlord still wouldn't give up. Gave us the equivalency of a 'fuck you.' The conglomerates wanted their pipeline, though, and they were paying the bills, so we find a village this guy controls, and we ground ourselves in, and we wait. We make it well known we're there. We bring in porn and beer and blast AC/DC all night, and the villagers, they're scared shitless and want left alone. They don't even like this guy, and they sure as hell don't like us, but they have no weapons, so they have no voice. They lack agency in the matter, I suppose, but we don't care because they're a means to an end. They're bait.

"A new convoy rolls into town, and we're ready for them. They never stand a chance. There are civilian casualties, because that's the shit that happens, but we keep killing fighters until one guy's left—the guy's brother. The brother says he hates this guy, and tells us we've killed everyone in the family except for him and who we're looking for, and he's willing to take us to him if we'll let him live.

"So we drive to another village, walk in with a gun pointed to the one brother's head, and they take us straight to the warlord. Dude's sitting in this room, looks like something out of 'Aladdin.' Hand-dyed carpets and little statues, literal stacks of cash everywhere, and he's got 10 guys protecting him while he's sitting on a throne." Woody laughed. "A goddamn throne.

"The first thing I do, when I see this shit, is I blow the brother's brains out, then me and the boys kill the guards. The guy, once the smoke has cleared, he's cowering behind his throne. I pull him out into the middle of the room and tell him he will let this pipeline get built, or he will die right there. He shakes his head and says 'never,' so I slit his throat, and he bleeds out all over this rug.

"My crew walks out, grabs a flight home, and an hour after we're back on American soil, we get paid and the pipeline gets built, and I drink until I black out and someone hires me for another gig. At any time in this process, this guy could have conceded and let the pipeline through and have made a few shekels from the deal, but the motherfucker had so much pride, he wouldn't let any Western dogs force him an inch. All these people died, and we wiped out this man's entire bloodline, so gas could be two cents cheaper on the gallon."

Woody finished the last of his coffee, set the cup on the table. He looked out the kitchen doorway. There wasn't anything interesting to see, but I don't think he was looking at anything that was there.

"My point is," he said, "is that sometimes you have to know when to let go."

He rested his fingertips on the envelope and pushed it across the table toward me.

JAMES D.F. HANNAH is the Shamus Award-winning author of the Henry Malone novels, as well as the novel *The Righteous Path*. A native of eastern Kentucky and southern West Virginia, Hannah was an award-winning former journalist and columnist before moving into governmental public relations. He lives with entirely too many cats in Louisville, Kentucky.

On the following pages are a few
more great titles from the
Down & Out Books publishing family.

For a complete list of books and to
sign up for our newsletter,
go to DownAndOutBooks.com.

Midnight Lullaby
A Henry Malone Crime Novel
James D.F. Hannah

Down & Out Books
January 2021
978-1-64396-171-2

A roadside shooting ended both his career and his marriage and sent ex-state trooper Henry Malone back to his childhood home in Serenity, West Virginia. A request to look into the disappearance of a young mother becomes a second chance, an opportunity to redeem himself.

But Malone finds the unexpected as he scratches beneath his hometown's surface: Crooked lawyers. Meth cooks. A hair-triggered sheriff. A beautiful legal secretary. And a seductive yet deadly white supremacist. It is a dangerous mix that leads Henry and his well-armed AA sponsor, Woody, down onto a wild and deadly road.

The Great Filling Station Holdup
Crime Fiction Inspired by the Songs of Jimmy Buffett
Josh Pachter, Editor

Down & Out Books
February 2021
978-1-64396-181-1

Editor Josh Pachter presents sixteen short crime stories by sixteen popular and up-and-coming crime writers, each story based on a song from one of the twenty-nine studio albums Jimmy has released over the last half century.

Including stories by Leigh Lundin, Josh Pachter, Rick Ollerman, Michael Bracken, Don Bruns, Alison McMahan, Bruce Robert Coffin, Lissa Marie Redmond, Elaine Viets, Robert J. Randisi, Laura Oles, Isabella Maldonado, Jeffery Hess, Neil Plakcy, John M. Floyd, and M.E. Browning.

Trigger Switch
Bryon Quertermous

All Due Respect, an imprint of
Down & Out Books
March 2021
978-1-64396-190-3

Dominick Prince has been a magnet for trouble his entire life. A series of poor life choices and their violent consequences have crushed his spirit. Desperate to outrun this burgeoning rage before it fully consumes him, Dominick accepts an offer he doesn't trust from an old high school classmate.

Dutchy Kent says he wants to make one last-ditch effort to prove his acting chops by mounting the New York City debut of a play based on one of Dominick's stories, but the true story involves the real estate empire of a notorious Queens drug dealer and $1.2 million in cash.

Deemer's Inlet
Stephen Burdick

Shotgun Honey, an imprint of
Down & Out Books
August 2020
978-1-64396-104-0

Far from the tourist meccas of Ft. Lauderdale and Miami Beach, a chief of police position in the quiet, picturesque town of Deemer's Inlet on the Gulf coast of Florida seemed ideal for Eldon Quick—until the first murder.

The crime and a subsequent killing force Quick to call upon his years of experience as a former homicide detective in Miami. Soon after, two more people are murdered and Quick believes a serial killer is on the loose. As Quick works to uncover the identity and motive of the killer, he must contend with an understaffed police force, small town politics, and curious residents.

Made in the USA
Coppell, TX
07 January 2023

10546858R20142